LOVE IN THE KINGDOM OF OIL

Nawal El Saadawi is an internationally renowned feminist writer and activist from Egypt. She is the founder and president of the Arab Women's Solidarity Association and co-founder of the Arab Association for Human Rights. Among her numerous roles in public office she has served as Egypt's National Director of Public Health and stood as a candidate in the 2004 Egyptian presidential elections. El Saadawi holds honorary doctorates from the universities of York, Illinois at Chicago, St Andrews and Tromso, and her numerous awards include the Council of Europe North-South Prize, the Women of the Year Award (UK), Sean MacBride Peace Prize (Ireland), and the National Order of Merit (France). She is the author of over fifty novels, short stories and non-fiction works centering on the status of Arab women, which have been translated into more than thirty languages.

'A formidable force in the
international world of literature'
New Humanist

'Egypt's foremost feminist writer ...
Saadawi writes beautifully'
Publishers Weekly

'Nawal El Saadawi writes with conviction,
humour and intelligence'
World Literature Today

NAWAL EL SAADAWI

Love in the Kingdom of Oil

Translated from Arabic by
Basil Hatim & Malcolm Williams

SAQI

SAQI BOOKS

26 Westbourne Grove
London W2 5RH
www.saqibooks.com

First published in English in 2001 by Saqi Books
This edition published 2019

Printed and bound by Clays Ltd, Elcograf S.p.A

A full CIP record for this book is available from the British Library

ISBN 978 0 86356 626 4
eISBN 978 0 86356 733 9

That day in September the news appeared in the newspapers. Half a line of poor quality newsprint run off by the printers:

WOMAN GOES ON LEAVE AND DOES NOT RETURN

It was a normal thing for people to vanish. Every day the sun came out and so did the newspapers. In some corner of an inside page was a personal column. The word 'personal' could be suppressed or replaced by another word, without changing anything at all. Personal. Persons. People. The people. The nation. The masses. Words that mean everything and nothing at the same time.

On the first page there was a coloured picture of His Majesty. Life size with a large title:

THE KING'S BIRTHDAY PARTY

People rubbed their eyes. The corners of their eyelids were careworn. They turned over page after page. They yawned until their jawbones cracked. The news appeared on an inside page, scarcely visible to the naked eye:

WOMAN GOES ON LEAVE AND DOES NOT RETURN.

Women do not go on leave. If one does, then she does so in order to run some essential errand. Before going, she must obtain written permission either in her husband's hand or stamped by her boss at work.

There is no precedent for a woman going and not returning. A man can go and not return for seven years, but only if he stays away longer than that does the wife have the right to free herself from him.

The police began actively to search for her. They put out leaflets and adverts in the newspapers seeking to find her, alive or dead, and announced a generous reward from His Majesty the King.

'What is the relationship between His Majesty the King and the disappearance of an ordinary woman?'

It almost goes without saying that nothing in the world can happen without an order from His Majesty, written or unwritten. His Majesty does not know how to read or write. That is a sort of privilege, because what is the point of reading and writing? The prophets did not know how to read and write, so is it possible for the King to be more virtuous than the prophets?

There was also the typewriter. It was an electric one. There was also a new, oil-powered typewriter. It wrote in all languages. Behind the typewriter there was a leather swivel-chair. On it sat a police commissioner. Above his head hung an enlarged picture of His Majesty the King in a gold frame, its borders replete with words from the sacred text.

'Has your wife happened to go on leave before?'

Her husband clamped his lips shut in silence. His eyes widened like someone suddenly awaking from sleep. He was wearing his sleeping attire and the muscles of his face hung limp. He rubbed his eyes with his fingertips and yawned. He was sitting on a wooden chair fixed firmly on the ground.

'No.'

'Did you have an argument?'

'No.'

'Has she ever previously left the conjugal home without your consent?'

'No.'

The investigation was taking place in a locked room. There was a red light hanging above the door indicating that nobody should enter. That way, there would be no leaks to the newspapers. The reports were kept inside a secret folder with a black cover. Written on it were the words: 'Woman goes on leave.'

The police commissioner was sitting on a swivel chair. He swivelled round so that his back was to the wall and the picture of His Majesty. Opposite him was the other chair fixed to the ground. On it was sitting another man, not her husband but her boss at work.

'Was she one of those women who are troublemakers and rebels against the established order?'

Her boss sat cross-legged. Between his lips was a black pipe that bent forward like the horn of a cow. His eyes stared upwards.

'No, she was a submissive woman in everyway.'

'Could she have been kidnapped or raped?'

'No. She was an ordinary woman who wouldn't arouse in anybody a desire to rape her.'

'What do you mean by that?'

'I mean that she was a passive woman who aroused nobody's passion.'

The police commissioner nodded his head indicating that he understood. He swivelled round in his chair so that his back was to her boss. He tapped with his fingers on the typewriter. A strange smell like burnt gas crept out. He stretched out his arm and adjusted the direction of the fan. Then he swivelled his chair round again.

'Do you think that she has run away?'

'Why should she run away?'

Nobody knows why a woman might run away. And if she has run away, where would she go? Could she have run away by herself?

'Do you think she ran away with another man?'

'Another man?'

'Yes.'

'Impossible. She was a totally honourable woman. Nothing occupied her apart from her work and her research.'

'Research?'

'She was working in the Research Section of the Archaeology Department.'

'Archaeology? What's that?'

'It means discovering remains of old civilizations by digging up the ground.'

'Like what?'

'Old statues of the ancient gods like Amun and Akhenaton, or the ancient goddesses like Nefertiti and Sekhmet.'

'Sekhmet? Who's that?'

'The ancient goddess of death.'

'May God protect us!'

A report came in from the inspector of a remote station. A woman had been seen climbing into a boat. On her shoulders hung a leather bag with a long strap. She looked like a student or a university researcher. She was all by herself without a man. Something was sticking out of her bag. It had an iron head tapering into a sort of chisel.

The police commissioner became on edge. Drops of sweat appeared on his forehead. He pressed on a black button and the speed of the fan increased. It had a neck that allowed it to rotate gradually. The air in the room was almost suffocating.

'Was the woman normal?'

On the nailed wooden chair sat a psychiatrist. His mouth was twisted towards the left, and the pipe with its stem curled like a horn tilting towards the right. His eyes stared at the upper half of the wall. The picture was in its gold frame. He exhaled a dense puff of smoke in the direction of His Majesty. Then he gave anxious attention to the policeman and turned his head in the other direction, where the fan was, and lowered his eyelids.

'I don't think she was a normal woman.'

'Are you referring to her research?'

'Yes. Usually a woman involved in matters outside the home is abnormal.'

'What do you mean?'

'A young woman throwing herself into a pointless job like collecting statues. Isn't that an indication of illness or even perversion?'

'Perversion?'

'That chisel reveals everything.'

'How's that?'

'In order to compensate for her unsatisfied desires, the woman takes enjoyment in burying the chisel in the ground as if it is a man's penis.'

The police commissioner shuddered on his chair. He spun round a number of times like the fan. His fingers froze on the typewriter as he typed the words 'penis'. He stopped typing and spun round with a swift movement.

'It appears to be a serious matter.'

'Indeed it is. I have written a number of pieces on this illness. From her childhood, the woman searches fruitlessly for the penis. And when she despairs of finding it, this desire changes into another desire.

'Another desire. Like what?'

'Like looking at herself in the mirror. A sort of narcissism.'

'May God protect us!'

'Such a woman has a tendency to isolate herself to keep silent and sometimes to steal.'

'To steal?'

'To steal rare artifacts and ancient statues. Especially ancient goddesses, for she is drawn towards people of her own sex and not the opposite one.'

'May God protect us!'

'At the same time, she is tempted with an urgent desire to disappear.'

'Disappear!?'

'In other words, a strong attraction towards suicide and death.'

'May God protect us!'

'In point of fact, when women look for archaeological remains, they feel great pleasure when they dig in the ground. They are drawn to the head of the chisel more than they are drawn to the head of the goddess Nefertiti. However much they try, they are unable to divert their eyes from the head of the chisel, as if it's the organ they desire.'

'Enough! Enough!'

The police commissioner was thoroughly perturbed. He

stopped breathing completely. Then he began to pant. The chair spun round incessantly. The chair came to a stop and he took up the bottle of correcting fluid. He began to erase the word 'penis' from all the papers. However, the news filtered out to the press in spite of the red lamp. The reporters began to write about the subject shamelessly. News of the woman who had disappeared almost diverted people's attention from the birthday celebrations of His Majesty the King.

The following day a royal decree was issued forbidding women to take leave and, if a woman did go on leave, it was forbidden to give her shelter or to conceal her.

* * *

That morning in September, a woman in the prime of youth went down to the landing stage. She had tied her thick black hair in two long plaits. She had wrapped the plaits three times around her head and they met above her forehead in a large bow. Her body was tall and slender inside a baggy gown that came down below her knees. Underneath it she was wearing a long baggy *sarwal*, the legs of which were tied above her feet. From her shoulder hung a bag with a long leather strap. She held it tightly by the strap, and strode along with her eyes looking up like someone about to set sail towards the boats of the sun. The station inspector had stared at her with a natural curiosity. At the gate he had seen her extend her hand to the inspector to show him her ticket. The inspector gazed at it for a moment then returned it to her. She moved swiftly out of the station. There was nothing in her movements to arouse suspicion except that enthusiasm, uncommon among women, which she displayed as she looked towards the sun, with eyes bare of any covering, and something like the head of a chisel sticking out of her bag.

Boats were at anchor beside the landing stage, as usual waiting for passengers, and the woman headed for one of them. She climbed in unhesitatingly and occupied a seat at the back.

The woman stayed in the boat until the terminus, disembarked with all the other passengers and walked away. Nature displayed a mixture of strange colours, rivalling into one another and blending. The green of the grass, the yellow of the desert, the rusty red of the rocks, the blue of the sky and the white of the clouds.

She continued to stride along, holding her bag by the strap that was hung over her shoulder, as if she was moving willy-nilly towards a definite destination.

There were no longer any villages or large stretches of cultivated land. Instead, there were scattered fields and thorn trees. Then the soil changed and became sort of desert-like, black and fine, mixed with dark red as if it had been immersed in blood and then dried off under the sun. It stuck to her feet as she walked. From time to time clumps of date palms cast their shadow on the ground, appearing as if by chance, a stark black stain in the midst of the sand.

The woman stopped in the shade of a wall, perhaps for the first time since she had disembarked from the boat. She wiped her face with the sleeve of her gown to dry the perspiration. She began to gaze around her. She took the leather strap off her shoulder and opened the bag. She held the chisel in her right hand, and the bag in her left and moved off quickly again. She shook the soil off her feet, striking her heels on the ground a number of times. In the distance a large stretch of black water glimmered, resembling a stagnant lake.

Then her gaze swung round, passing over a low hill. A little village appeared, with houses made of black mud or some substance looking like mud, all huddled together. On the roofs were piles of garbage and upturned jars. The alleys were narrow and ended in cul-de-sacs. And then there was a large expanse of bare ground.

On the horizon was the top of a hill. The village stretched out below it. Massive pipes tore through it, gushing with what looked like black water. There were also wide-mouthed wells from which flowed a liquid resembling mercury; there was the smell of gas mixed with that of human beings, and something like salted sardines or kippers, and dead dogs on the dirt road that had been knocked down by vehicles speeding through the night.

The dirt road went downhill and the woman followed it. She walked fast, heading towards her goal, her bag slung over her shoulder by the strap. The village children were playing in a lake in front of the mosque. Old men were squatting on the bare ground, gazing fixedly at their toes and from time to time raising their eyes to heaven and gazing into space. A long string of women hidden under black abayas walked along slowly with jars on their heads.

The women stopped moving and watched the woman. Their eyes sparkled through little slits. But the woman went on her way with the chisel in her hand, thinking of nothing except her research. She stopped a moment to wipe away the sweat with the sleeve of her gown and gazed around her. The pipes wound away endlessly, and the road descended to the lake. She took out of her bag a small map that she looked at for a long time, then raised clouded eyes to heaven. At that moment a little girl from the village passed by. She was wearing a black *abaya* and nothing was visible of her apart from two little eyes. The woman asked her the way, but the child shivered and moved away quickly. Confusion appeared on her face, and she became perturbed.

The view stretched away to the horizon and some birds hovered. The movement of their wings and the blue of the sky behind them brought some of her confidence back. The road in front of her appeared to be firm, but the ground became increasingly damp and soft under her feet. The village appeared to plunge into the depths of the lake.

From the place where she had stopped, she gazed around her. What village was this? She moved her feet to continue on her way but a sudden gust of wind came along and almost snatched her off the ground. It would have done so had she not dug in her feet and caught hold of a wall, which began to shake under the weight of her body.

She straightened up to the sound of voices muttering. She saw the child standing a long way off talking to another little girl. They put their heads together and looked in her direction. The woman wanted to call and ask them the name of the village. She called out in a loud voice. She saw them turn round, then realised from their bent backs that they were two old ladies.

She looked at her watch. It was ten past seven. She beat the ground with her chisel and a question occurred to her, 'Was it really possible for goddesses to live underground, or could that not be simply a ploy to draw her to this place?'

She closed her eyes as if asleep. She saw the square room with its corners bare of furniture and the wooden double bed with a pale yellow cover on it. There was a stain of old blood on the cover. There was a shelf on which there were some books about archaeology, a small stone statuette of the one-breasted god and a picture of the god Akhenaton with two prominent breasts and two large buttocks.

From behind the smoke of his pipe, her boss would steal a glance at her. He believed that the male god could have a breast or two but he did not believe in the existence of goddesses, and if there ever happened to be one, she would be the wife of a god and not a goddess in her own right.

Her male and female colleagues in the department believed the same as their boss did. They had come to the archaeology department in despair. They pursed their lips when they pronounced the word *archaeology*. They were attracted by mummies more than by living beings. Their eyes dropped as if gravitating to the depths of the earth. They walked in almost the same way. Their necks appeared twisted and their eyelids hung over their eyes. They had beak-like noses and fat dangling buttocks from sitting long hours behind a desk.

She lifted her eyes to heaven. She saw stars and planets fixed in the places that they had occupied ever since she was a child. Her aunt had pointed at a star so far away that she could scarcely see it. That one's Mars, and there are Mercury, Jupiter and Saturn. And that one over there is the mistress of them all, Venus.

★ ★ ★

Her eyes were fixed on the star. Suddenly the movement began. Venus moved from its place and crossed the heavens. Its tail stretched behind it long and slender. Then the stars began to move away from one another, moving here and there and taking on the appearance of animals. There was a star resembling the bull, the lion, the whale and the scorpion.

The earth also began to move under her feet. She gazed around her. A man was walking a long way away with his back bent and his head wrapped in a white headcloth.

'Is it an earthquake, uncle?'

'No, it's the bull shaking his horns and tossing the earth from horn to horn.'

The man's voice was as clear as if he was speaking directly in her ear. Nevertheless, it seemed as if it came from the bottom of a well. He was walking slowly away and all she could see of him was his bent back. He gradually disappeared in a cloud of mist.

She called out to him at the top of her voice, but her cry dissipated.

Then a muffled laugh rang out. It was the childlike old lady standing in her *abaya*. Her little eyes sparkled from inside their slits.

'It's not the bull, sister.'

'What is it?'

The diminutive old woman disappeared in a cloud of smoky dust. The woman stood with her feet fixed to the ground. She held the strap of the bag and began to pull on it. All she could do was stand firm in the face of the crazed movement of the earth.

She raised her eyes to the horizon. Expanses of black stretched in front of her like an endless desert. The sand was moving, black in colour, and the wind was very dry. The surface of her tongue was cracked and her eyes were searching in the darkness for a drop of water. She noticed something moving, a small snake resembling a chameleon. Its eyes sparkled as it crawled along in its black skin. Its movements were graceful and its steps light and joyful as if it was rejoicing in its ability to change colour.

Her hold on the strap of her bag relaxed. Perhaps standing firm was not what was required. She abandoned herself to the wind, an attitude that her body was not used to at first. It appeared to be heavy. Then it became lighter. She closed her eyes in something resembling surrender. A new sensation began to flow into her, one of embarrassment. It was hot. At every step, black dust stuck to her shoes. She stopped for a moment. She knocked her heals against one another. She undid her plaits from around her head. She shook them out. She knocked one against another. Black particles flew around her, sticking to her nose and her forehead as if attracted by the smell of sweat.

She squatted without letting her bottom touch the ground. She did not want to dirty her cloak. She opened the bag and took out the chisel. She struck the ground a number of times, but the smell was unbearable. She put a handkerchief over her nose. Her neck was bent downwards. The earth stretched in front of her, and the darkness was becoming thicker. She was walking down the slope. Anybody who saw her would not have thought that she was walking. Her hand bumped into a mud wall. It resembled the walls of the village houses. She heard voices inside. She was standing, resting her hand on the wall. Her other hand held onto the chisel, and she was panting.

A door opened in the wall. It made a noise like the squeaking of a water wheel, rusty metal hinges or the creaking of old wood. A young woman appeared in a black *abaya*, carrying on her head a massive earthenware jar with a bloated stomach. The skin on her hands was cracked. Her feet were large and shod in leather shoes. The colour of her heels appeared to be black. Her head was wrapped in a black scarf tied in a knot above her forehead. The earthenware jar on her head was tilted, filled up to the brim, on the verge of toppling but not actually doing so. She twisted and turned her head without holding the jar with her hand, but not a drop of water escaped from it.

The woman was gazing at the chisel in her hand. She had never in her life seen a woman carrying a sharp instrument. She took a step back.

'It's only a chisel.'

'What's that, sister?'

'I dig up the ground with it and search for goddesses.'

'What?'

'The goddess Sekhmet for instance.'

'Sekhmet!?'

The woman was overcome with perturbation. Her body began to shake. But the jar remained fixed in its place, sitting composedly on her head.

'Give me a little water please ...'

'What?'

'Water ... water ...' she repeated, beginning to scream. The woman stood staring at her through the slits, wide-eyed, as if she was watching a sheep bleat. At that moment there was another gust of wind, which almost tore her from the ground. The woman stood shaking her head, with the jar sitting firmly on it.

'Who are you?'

She saw doubt in the woman's eyes. She took her identity card out of her bag: name, sex, eye colour; profession: researcher in the archaeology department; of spotless reputation, married, no children. Her confidential files were unsullied. Her insurance premiums and taxes had all been paid. She had no debts and no police record. And until now no judgements had been issued against her.

The woman gazed at the identity card as if she did not know how to read. She considered her photograph, which was fastened with a pin.

'Why don't you veil your face? Have you no shame?'

She returned the identity card to her and then turned away. She walked slowly away down the track. She sucked with her lips and clicked her leather shoes. Her black heels kicked the dust into the air. On her back was a protrusion resembling the hump of a camel. Around her had gathered other women with jars on their heads. They all put their heads together. Whispered mutterings went round the group. One of them jumped up. From afar it appeared to be the diminutive one. A moment later she returned surrounded by a number of men. They were wearing baggy jallabas. On their heads were white headcloths.

The voices of the women remained a low hum, no more than a whisper. The men's voices rose. They were all speaking at the same time, moving their arms in the air, beating the ground with their feet. A thick cloud of dust arose. Then the voices all suddenly stopped and silence fell. All that could be heard was the barking of a dog a long way off. She turned to go on her way. She quickened her pace. However, the voices followed her. A man with a black *keffiyeh* round his neck ordered her to stop. On his face were black spots like freckles.

'You, woman!'

The word 'woman' pierced her ears like a sliver of glass. The muscles of her face stiffened. What gave a man the right to order her to stop by the side of the bridle path and then pour invective upon her? She turned her back on him and continued on her way. He followed her, beating the ground with his feet. His voice never stopped repeating that ugly word.

He stretched out his long arm like a wooden staff and seized her arm. He put his mouth to her ear and cried, 'Woman!' A pungent smell erupted from his mouth and a stream of black saliva escaped from the side of it. 'Who are you?'

'I am a respectable researcher and ...'

'Where are you from?'

She turned round and signalled with her head to the track from which she had come. It looked like a long dark subterranean vault, blotted out by black waters from the flood. She shut her eyes and then opened them.

'I went on leave and ...'

'We've never heard of such a thing.'

'Can I go back?'

'There is no way of going back at this time.'

'Can I rent a room until the morning?'

'Are you alone?'

The man shook his head a number of times. 'It's impossible.'

He walked away from her, beating the ground with his feet.

She opened the bag and took out the map. Had she mistaken the place? She crouched down on the ground. To anyone watching her from afar she looked like someone about to sleep. However, she was deep in thought, trying to determine where she was. She came across a spot, which she marked with a pencil. She took hold of the chisel and began to dig.

Her head hung down as she dug, as if she was worn out. Perhaps it was the right place; perhaps a goddess was buried here. However, the darkness was total, and black specks danced in front of her eyes. She cleared away the dirt and noticed something like an ox's horn. Before she could stretch out her arm she heard voices behind her. A line of men wearing *jallabas* were looking down at her. Their heads were wrapped in white headgear. Behind them was a line of women in their black *abayas*. One of them exposed her bare breast from under her *abaya*, and began to press on the black teat between her fingers until a thin white stream emerged from the opening. Then she took a little child from under her *abaya*. It took hold of the teat between its little jaws and began to suckle audibly.

The voices of the men became as faint as the voices of the women. They squatted on the ground forming a little circle. In the middle of a large stone sat their chief. On his little finger glittered a ring and above his head was a picture of His Majesty. The picture was surrounded by coloured lamps and a loudspeaker like a funnel.

'On the occasion of His Majesty's birthday we have been commanded to spend lavishly.'

The voice was the voice of His Majesty. His lips moved in the picture. They rubbed their eyes with their fingers. The corners of their eyelids were wrinkled and bloodshot. They exchanged glances, and repeated with one voice, 'able to do all things'. Then silence fell. They all rubbed their eyes, and considered the little black specks sticking to their fingertips. They wiped them off with their *jallabas* and then rubbed their eyes again.

The voice of His Majesty mumbled over the loudspeaker. His words were indistinct, spoken in a strange accent, and nobody understood what he was saying. Their leader shook his head as a sign of pleasure and they all shook their heads. Then his head stopped shaking and their heads stopped shaking too. He jumped up from his seat, and they all jumped up too. He disappeared into the darkness of the night, and the men all disappeared behind him, and behind them went the women.

All that remained was the picture of His Majesty, hung in the sky without columns, and above it the trumpet. One man was sweeping the ground. He approached her slowly. He was the man with the freckles and the black *keffiyeh*. He blew his nose loudly.

'This place must be cleared.'

'And where shall I sleep?'

'Come with me.'

He led her to the track going downhill. He went a pace or two ahead of her. Whenever she speeded up to walk near him, he would let his eyes rest on her, and she would slow down so that she was once more behind him. He went down the incline with his torso leaning forward, scratching his back with his hand.

She followed him with the strap of the bag over her shoulder, holding on to it with her fingers as if it would protect her from falling. In her other hand was the chisel, vibrating in unison with her body, but in the darkness appearing as if it was vibrating by itself.

The track went downhill and the soil became damper. The pungent smell increased. Her legs sank in up to her knees. The man gathered up his *jallaba* and tied it round his waist. Then he jumped into a boat. She jumped in behind him and the boat rocked. She would have fallen if she had not regained her balance with a movement of her arm.

The scene appeared natural to her, apart from the pungent smell and the flying black particles that penetrated her nose and ears and stuck to the corners of her eyelids. Darkness piled up in front of her eyes like hills, and the silence weighed down on her, relieved only by the sound of the oar striking the endless black sea.

The man began to rub his eyes as he sang,

O giver of life,
O taker of the spirit,
Mercifully spare us from the flood,
O deliverer from all anxieties.

As he sang, his eyes gazed towards the horizon. He rubbed the corner of his eye with his fingertip then looked closely at his finger and considered it for a long time before wiping it on his *jallaba*. Then he began to rub his back, under his armpit and between his thighs. The sound of his song floated sadly in the night, apart from the occasional moments when his voice quickened with sudden pleasure.

He stopped the boat at a mass of darkness resembling a wall. He leant forward in the direction of the darkness. He cleared his throat loudly to announce his arrival. All that could be heard was the barking of the dog. As he rapped on the door, he cried out, 'Open up, brother.'

From behind the door another man could be heard clearing his throat. From the depths of the darkness, the door opened. A smell gushed out which hurt the membrane of her nose. A small flame appeared, trembling in a large hairy hand, and a rattling voice emerged from a throat, 'Come in, woman.'

The word no longer pained her. A greater pain was in her ears. The tiny particles were building up inside both ears. They were becoming hard like little bits of gravel that rubbed on the membrane or the nerve.

His voice rose slightly, 'Come in, woman.'

She was standing in her place without any part of her moving apart from her neck, which was turned upwards towards heaven, seeking air. Over her shoulder she pulled on the strap as if pulling her memory out of the darkness. How had she come here?

His voice rose even more, 'Can't you hear what is being said to you?'

She moved her feet and entered. She passed over a low threshold with a familiar shape. However, the house rocked under her feet as if it were a boat. The door closed behind her and she turned round. The man with the black freckles was not there. She heard the sound of the oars moving away. The man burst into staccato coughs then blew his nose loudly. She withdrew a step. In her anxiety it appeared as if she was returning to her childhood and she let out a cry. The light was so faint that she could scarcely see anything. She rubbed her eye with her fingertip. The room was bare of furniture and there was a chair nailed to the ground. Doubt overcame her. Had she never left her place?

'Take off your clothes.'

His voice was no longer strange to her ears. The wind was rattling the window. Threads of black liquid were pushing their way in under the door. Black drops like rain were falling from the ceiling.

In point of fact, there was no window. It was simply planks of wood. And the floor was not a floor but rather planks of wood creaking under her feet like sick cats. A dampness like sweat crept out of the planks, sticking to the heels of her shoes, or the soles of her feet if she took off her shoes.

'The smell is unbearable!'

She put a handkerchief over her nose and closed her eyes. His voice was rattling and distant as if coming from the other world. All that she could see of him were his feet and his knees inside his nightshirt. His upper half was hidden behind the newspaper. Black lead-print letters, line after line, poured out in tiny horizontal lines:

Researchers wanted in the Archaeology Department.

★ ★ ★

She typed out the request on the typewriter. She filled in the boxes for name, age and religion. In the box marked sex, she typed 'female'. The head of department looked at her wide-eyed, 'This department only accepts males. The work we do, I mean digging up the ground, is not suitable.'

'My aunt used to dig up the ground, and my mother also used to dig up the ground, and sow and ...'

'Digs are something else ... I mean searching for gods in the bowels of the earth.'

'The gods are in heaven, are they not?'

'But there are other gods. Haven't you read anything about archaeology?'

She noticed something crawling under her foot. A long soft finger, like the tale of a snake. It was twisting and turning and digging a tunnel for itself after coming down from the roof. There was also a trickle of black liquid. Round it gathered hordes of ants, geckos, lizards, and cockroaches looking like scarabs with wings, which beat with something resembling joy.

She heard his voice from behind the newspaper. He was speaking to himself or reading a headline in an audible voice. Some movement crept into that room which was plunged in such darkness. Those little wings shed some joy as they hovered around the lamp. She stretched her legs over the low seat. Her feet were swollen from all the walking she had done, and the skin, covered in a layer of black grime, was peeling. Her bag was over her shoulder, dangling from the strap. The chisel was inside the bag, of course. Her eyes gazed around her, exploring the place. On top of the black wall she saw it again. A black lizard or a chameleon. It gazed at her with little eyes. A friendship was growing up between them.

The man cleared his throat loudly. The lizard hid in the crack. She did not know how he had seen it from behind the newspaper. His top half was hidden completely. Only his feet and his knees were visible through his nightshirt. Perhaps they were feelers that were apprehensive of any friendship that might spring up between her and another being.

'Get the dinner ready, said he in the tone of someone who had hired a woman to cook for him. There was no space for that in the form she had typed on the typewriter. In the space marked work, she had already written 'Researcher into goddesses'. 'I'm hungry!' he cried again in a loud voice.

In the kitchen the window was blocked. Here too, wooden boards had been nailed in, and bits of newspaper had been stuck in the cracks and piled up behind the door to prevent the trickle from entering under the door. The water tap was also blocked with newspaper.

As she was standing in front of the sink, she sensed the man behind her. She felt his breath on the back of her neck. She did not know how to light the match, so he gave her something like a revolver. She pressed on it with her thumb; it cracked, and a spark flew out. She laughed like a child.

Little things used to make her laugh. The darkness dispersed and a light shone on the horizon. She saw him bend his head upwards with pride. She followed his glance to the ceiling with her eyes. The black trickle was continuing to advance.

'What's that?'

'Don't you know what it is?'

'No.'

'It's the oil.'

'Does the oil seep through the ceiling?'

'Of course, when the level rises in the ground or it pours down from the sky.'

'Does the sky rain it down as well?'

'The sky gives what it wants boundlessly.'

When she was in school as a child, she had learnt that oil is only found in the bowels of the earth. Over millions of years, it had been generated from dead bodies that disintegrated because of the heat, and little organisms called bacteria, and particles of soil and sand, and mineral dust. All that disintegrated into minute particles that absorbed water, and was stored in sponge-like layers, into which ran sand and little fragments of limestone. It was caught among the little particles and stored in cracks between two insulating layers, one that prevented it seeping upwards and the other a layer of water in the depths of the earth on which it floated, and which prevented it seeping lower. Like a prey for which all exits are closed, preventing it from emerging to the surface of the earth. Unless of course it should be shaken by an earthquake, a volcano or a bomb dropped in war.

She pursed her lips in silence. His neck was still craned upwards addressing the sky as if it was a goddess. She raised her head and he caught it from behind. He was standing behind her, rubbing against her without shame. She cringed inside her body in anguish. There was no box in the work contract for such things. Her cringing filled his soul with confidence, and he clung to her more. His breathing brushed her neck from behind. His arm stretched out and encircled her chest. Then his hand came to rest on her left breast. She saw his black nails from which emanated the smell of oil.

'Aren't you going to take a shower first?'

'What?'

His anger showed. Never before had a woman been as daring as this. His hand almost rose and fell on her face. Perhaps it did really rise. Then he took a step back, suddenly seized by exhaustion. He pointed to a little glass on a wooden shelf. He opened his mouth so wide that she could see the red uvula vibrating in his throat.

'Four drops.'

She poured four drops down his throat. He closed his eyes for a long time, then he opened them. She licked her lower lip with the end of her tongue.

'Is it water?'

'No. They are a sort of oil drops, which quench the thirst more than water, and cleanse the intestines. Open your mouth.'

He poured into her mouth the first drop and then the second. She wanted the third and the fourth drop. She clung to the bottle, holding it with all five fingers, but he wrenched it from her and concealed it. 'According to the law you only get two drops'.

She bowed her head. She was in a state of dazed exhaustion. It was as if she had heard about this law before. She fell asleep and saw herself taking a shower in warm water. The sky was pure blue and the fields were green. In her nostrils was the smell of farmland. She was sitting on the bridge at sunset waiting for the lights to appear.

She opened her eyes to the sensation of something burning under her eyelid. The room was bathed in darkness. A faint light was emitted by a lamp that burned languidly. He was sitting in his place behind the open newspaper. His feet were bare on the tiles.

She tucked her bag under her arm. She began to drag her feet to the kitchen. She came back with a cup of black tea. He stretched out his arm and took the cup without saying anything, and sank into something resembling sleep. The newspaper was rolled up into a ball on the ground. She opened it and turned it page by page. 'A woman has gone on leave and has not returned. According to the law it is forbidden to give her shelter or to conceal her.'

Noiselessly, she hung the bag over her shoulder. She closed the door cautiously and went out. The wind howled like a hungry wolf. Her feet sank in at every step. She could not tell the mud from the dry ground. She used the walls for support as she used to do when she was a little girl, before she learnt to walk, with her aunt holding her hand.

One, two, buckle your shoe.
Three, four, walk to the door.
Help her, our Lady of Purity.

When she was a little girl, she did not know who the Lady of Purity was. Perhaps it was the Virgin Mary. In the darkness of the night, her face sometimes used to hover over the roofs of the village. Some blind people had their sight restored and movement was restored to some paralysed legs. Or perhaps it was Lady Zaynab, the only prophet who was able to heal her aunt of pain.

'What are you saying?'

'I will be a prophet … so that I can heal people.'

'Have you lost your mind? There are no female prophets.'

His voice rang clearly in her ears. It dispersed her dreams. The voice of a man. Perhaps it was her husband or her boss. In the entrance examination he was sitting behind his desk, with a black pipe between his lips, which shook as he asked her question after question.

'What do you know about Numu, the first goddess of the waters?'

'Numu?'

'And Inana, the goddess of nature and fertility?'

'Inana?'

'And Sekhmet, the goddess of death?'

She did not know that there were such things as goddesses. The prophets were all men, and there was not a woman among them. How then could there be female gods? Which are higher in rank, prophets or gods? As for the god of death, his name was Ezra'el not Sekhmet, and he was male not female.

She was reading in the light of the lamp. He was sitting in his usual place. His top half was hidden behind the newspaper.

'Are you reading?'

All that was visible of him were his feet and legs. His angular knees stuck out from under his nightshirt. Were his eyes in his knees? She no sooner opened her book and started to read than she could see them shaking – was it in irritation?

'Leave the book.'

'The exam is tomorrow. I haven't finished revising and …'

'I'm hungry.'

She looked at the watch on her wrist. Ten past nine. She had prepared him his food an hour previously. How could he get hungry again so quickly? And if he was hungry, the saucepan was on the stove, and the kitchen was only three paces away. She saw him sitting down shaking his knees and moving his feet in the air, cracking his toes.

'I'm thirsty.'

He never stopped making demands. Like a child, he could neither feed himself nor get himself something to drink. He would no sooner see her opening a book than he would shout. As if the book was another man who was taking her from him.

She hid the book under the pillow. She would wait until he was asleep, sound asleep, and his snoring had begun to rise and fall regularly. She opened the book and read. In it there were commands from the mother goddess to her daughter:

'Do not forget your mother.'

'Bear her as she bore you.'

'She bore you in her stomach for a whole year.'

'She gave you her life and died.'

In the quietness of the night, the voice rang in her ears. She had never heard the voice of her mother except when she was a foetus in the womb. She saw him turning over in his sleep as if he heard the voice. His hairs bristled in irritation. He opened his eyes suddenly and she hid the book. He rolled over on his other side and went back to sleep. She lay in her place waiting. She did not know if he was sleeping or pretending to sleep. His breathing had not grown louder yet and the rise and fall of his snoring was not regular.

'Are you awake?'

She closed her eyes and pursed her lips. She let her breathing rise and fall. Then she fell asleep. Her body was falling down and down as if into a well.

***

Everything was becoming damp, even the bed covers. A black dampness with a pungent smell. She saw him kneeling down on his hands and feet. Then he stretched out his arm towards her. He began to gaze into her face without changing his position. His lips hung open in an unnatural fashion, and the hair on his chest was exposed.

She realised that he was determined to go ahead with this game. So her muscles contracted, and she purposefully locked up her body. She pursed her lips and pretended to sleep.

The black liquid poured down even more profusely with a sound like a waterfall. It came up to his knees as he sat there. He jumped up, his body sluggish, yawning. He rubbed his eyes. He blew his nose in the basin. He brought a ladle from the kitchen. He began to ladle it up from the ground. He bent over until his torso stretched downwards. He filled the ladle and raised it with his arms, at the same time raising his torso. He emptied it in the jar. He filled jar after jar without stopping.

'The level is rising awfully fast'

'All good things come from God.'

'I'm suffocating.'

'Don't stand around like that. Get down on your knees.'

He made her kneel down like a camel. He wrung out an old rag, then folded it into a circle and placed it on her head. He fastened it with a succession of blows as if he was banging a nail into a wall. He bent over from his waist, planting his feet firmly on the ground. He raised the jar with his arms, then placed it on her head. Her neck bent under the weight. The jar almost fell. The wind blew and the jar tilted sideways.

She left it tilting and moved her feet, one after the other. She moved in the normal way along the path in front of her, as if she had walked along it before. She was familiar with this line of women, and she was one in the line. They moved with slow firm steps like those of time. The storm increased and the waterfall roared. Their bodies shook like straw blown by a gust of wind. Everything shook, apart from the jars on their heads, which remained fixed sedately in their places.

She used to return with her body exhausted. She would curl up on the ground, her knees under her chin and her bag under her head. Her throat was dry and her tongue was cracked. She opened her eyes in the darkness. She looked for the glass bottle. It wasn't anywhere. She went back to sleep. Then she woke up to a noise. He had caught an animal like a sheep or a goat. He had slaughtered it with a knife. The blood was pouring out like a fountain. The eyes looked towards her, as if they had never seen her before, and his voice roared, 'Hey, you. Come and cook.'

'I don't eat meat.'

'You don't have to eat it. All you have to do is cook it!'

'I won't cook it.'

He stretched out his long arm with the knife. She looked at the shining blade and bent her neck down. She cringed inside her body, hiding her neck with her hands.

She dragged her body sluggishly to the kitchen. She wiped away the blood around her neck, lit the gas and put on the saucepan. Steam rose to the ceiling. She felt him standing behind her. He was savouring the aroma of the meat, and rubbing up against her from behind. When the appetite for food was aroused in him, other appetites of his were aroused as well. She abandoned her body to him and went off to sleep.

As she was sleeping she felt a pain. Her conscience was pricking her. How could I give him myself in return for supper?

In the morning there was a violent gust of wind. On the crest of the wind a sound came to her like that of an oar. She listened carefully, her heart beating. She heard a woman's voice like that of her aunt.

The sound was dissipated when the man moved his eyelids. He pulled her up and the black pupil appeared, staring at her. He seized an old rag, perhaps her *sarwal*. He began to twist it between his hands as if he was ringing it out. He made it into a cord, which he placed on her head. He made her bend over from the waist and then raised the jar with one hand.

'It's very heavy! It'll break my neck.'

Her voice came back to her as if she was speaking to herself. She carried it along the street towards the company, as if in a dream. Perhaps for this reason, her body was strong. She was able to carry it without getting tired. Rather she felt a type of lightness like one feels in dreams. But her heart was heavy. Even a self-respecting ox would refuse this sort of work. Perhaps the only creature who would accept it would be some extinct species of donkey. The jar also was of an extinct type. It had two ears and a stomach bloated in pregnancy like the one-breasted god.

Some sounds echoed from afar. Faint cries uttered in unison, followed by sounds of muttering, muffled laughter, and then silence.

It seemed to her that she was walking without moving forward even a single step. She was standing where she had been. She was no more than two paces from the threshold of the house. The door was open and he was sitting on his seat behind the newspaper.

'The storm continues.'

'You can wait.'

'In this situation?'

'When the oil begins to creep over the ground, nothing can stand in its way. You must deal with it when the sun is shining and it has dried.'

'This jar is making my head hot!'

'There's nothing to do but wait, nothing.'

As he said the word 'nothing', he looked upwards. A grey cloud was twisting round and round on the skyline.

'The oil is drinking the water vapour in the air. When the clouds are dispersed by the sun, drought results.'

'Drought?'

'Yes, the liquid disappears, changing into solid, and you can walk on it easily without your feet sinking into it. Even tanks can cross it.'

When he said 'tanks', his eyes began to glisten as if with tears. Perhaps they would take him off to the war. His space on the bed would become empty and she would stop cooking. She tensed the muscles of her throat under the weight of the jar. She beat the ground with her feet.

The man was busy looking at the path. The vanguard of the great procession had appeared. A line of people carrying drums beating out the national anthem. Swarms of motorbikes and fireworks, employees of the palace inside long black cars, followed by the journalists. A vast tank out of which leant His Majesty, waving with his hands as if to the masses. Beside him was the president of the company, raising his hat in greeting.

She was walking along, the road empty in front of her, when the bamboo cane stung her on her rump.

'Bow quickly!'

She did not know yet how to pay her respects. She leant forwards from the waist and bent the top of her trunk backwards. She became like a camel in the process of kneeling down. The man began to teach her the anthem. His voice intoned a song in a quiet semi-musical voice. After every syllable he would dry his sweat with the sleeve of his *jallaba*.

'Is it the national anthem?'

'Yes, here we follow the principle "I love my country."'

'Is it your country?'

'My mother was buried here, and where your mother is buried, that's where your country is.'

He said the word 'country' and bowed to the ground. He lowered his eyelids over his eyes as if to conceal tears. He never mentioned his mother except when threatened by death. In his hands he held a small piece of paper stamped with the face of His Majesty, and an immediate summons.

She lay down with her eyes open, straining her ears to hear. She felt him climbing into bed beside her. He turned his face to the wall. She stretched out her arm and stroked his neck from behind. 'Don't go, for all you've got left there is your mother's tomb.'

'Anybody who doesn't go is killed.'

'And whoever goes is killed.'

'There is no escape from death.'

'Then let's die as and when we want to.'

She said it soundlessly as she got out of bed. She hung her bag over her shoulder and took hold of the chisel. She walked swiftly, squinting her eyes in the face of the storm. Her feet sank into the black water up to her knees. Movement seemed impossible. She stopped, piercing the darkness with her eyes and straining her ears to listen. At first the voices were faint.

Like the rustling of the wind or the flapping of *jallabas*. It came from the bottom of the slope where the houses of the village were, and gradually climbed up the slope. It resembled the beating of tambourines and the throbbing of drums. She saw a woman spinning round on one foot. Around her the women formed a circle, their hair ruffled. Their teeth chattered and they had their arms outstretched. They beat the ground with their feet, spinning round like the earth does. They were singing with one voice:

Our lady of purity,
Lighten our burdens.

The woman in the middle was tall, her head tied with a black scarf. She was like her aunt, beating the ground with her feet. She lifted her eyes to heaven as if entreating the mother goddess. At every spin her body shook. Her movements became increasingly fast and light. At the climax of the last paroxysm, her body became so light that it appeared to disintegrate. Time stopped and silence fell. Then movement broke out once again. It overflowed towards the ocean, and the women's bodies shook.

Our Lady of Purity,
Deliver us from the flood.

It was as if it was an old chant that the girls used to sing in school. Her lips opened and she began to whisper the song. But the words froze on her lips as torches pierced the darkness. She closed her eyes and could hear nothing apart from the barking of dogs. Metal wheels beat the ground. The women hid, concealing their hair under black scarves. The only person who remained was the tall woman who had been in the middle. The men surrounded her and carried her to the van. One cry and then silence reigned.

She didn't know how she returned to the house. Her eyelids were stuck together. She rubbed the corners of her eyes with her fingertips. She saw black particles like mist. Around her a waterfall was gushing. The pungent smell in her nostrils brought her back to reality. Everything was dreamlike. The one definite movement was the movement of the oil. A strange movement, which appeared to be the opposite of any other movement.

The man had returned from the war with one arm. In the morning he went out to fill the jar. When he raised his arm, it appeared thin and emaciated, as if it had lost half of its weight. It shook in the wind, rising and falling in an endless movement. Like someone bailing water out of the sea.

'Vanity! Vanity!' She spoke in an inaudible voice. Her neck bent under the load. The movement of his arm as he bailed out the oil resembled the movement of her neck as she carried the jar. She stopped in her place like an unruly stallion. She planted her feet on the ground. But stopping appeared impossible. The oil was pouring out, and it was in liquid form. Light bodies could float on it. If her body was light she could swim. However, she had not learnt how to float on water. Before she went into the sea, she had to take off her clothes, and women should not take off their clothes.

She closed her eyes without knowing the time. She looked at her watch with her eyelids locked closed. Then she remembered that she could not find out the time without opening her eyes. She pressed her eyelids together, then opened half an eye. It was ten past five. On the horizon there were faint rays of light; she did not know if they signalled dawn or dusk.

She began to get up from her bed. Before she moved, she wanted to make sure that the man was sound asleep. She began to put one foot in front of the other noiselessly. The man turned over on the other side and went back to sleep. She contemplated him for a long time. Curled up in a ball like an orphan child. Surrendered to sleep in what seemed to be despair. She bent low over him as if she would plant a goodbye kiss on his forehead. What would he say about her when he woke up and did not find her? Her conscience was still alive, or so she imagined. A goodbye kiss would not cause her any trouble anyway.

She opened the door and went out. She went forward a few steps and the earth became softer. Her feet sank in up to her knees. She succeeded in pulling out her right leg and then her left. Then she retraced her steps panting.

The man was sitting with head bowed as if in sadness. Her eyes filled with longing for him as if with tears. 'I tried to run away but I couldn't move.'

The man kept quiet without moving.

'I can't remain here!' She stood stiffly and her voice choked. The man's silence and his bent head took on a frightening meaning. Would her fate be tied to his fate forever?

The sun had risen in the sky. Its rays flared up with a red colour. Some corners of the lake caught fire. Smoke arose, concealing the sky and the disk of the sun. He raised his head, rubbing his eyes. 'This smoke is a kindness from God, for it reduces the temperature.'

His voice no longer stirred her body with waves of anger. On her face was drawn an expression of despair. She was standing barefoot with her head dangling over her chest. The bones of her body dangled in surrender and the strap of the bag dangled over her shoulder. 'Yes, resistance is meaningless.'

Her voice sounded exhausted and almost inaudible. The man could not hear it either. His bent head had some humanity in it. Some emotion tied her to him. It was certainly not love.

His feet suddenly slipped and he fell on his face. She helped him to get up, brushing the dust off him. But he pushed her away, and the muscles of his face contracted.

'If you hadn't been standing like this, I wouldn't have fallen over.'

'Your foot slipped.'

'It wasn't my foot!'

'If it wasn't your foot, what was it?'

'You! You standing in my way like this.'

She was standing far away from him. Whatever had happened, she could not be the cause of his falling down. However, he was unable to grasp any other reason. He believed in the following principle: 'If misfortune struck him, it was because of a woman. If good came his way, it was because of himself.'

She did not utter a single word. She held her head in her hands. She had to pretend that his foot had not slipped. She was the cause of his falling down. She had to apologise for stepping out, and to ask his forgiveness.

She curled up at his feet. Her eyes looked at him as he stood there. She stopped moving completely. She pretended to be dead for a moment. Then she woke up. The waterfall was gushing away, drowning everything. However, the people of the village were going on their way as if nothing was happening. The voices of newspaper vendors arose. He was standing without a sound. The silence confirmed that everything was clear without words. The jar was in front of her, the lake behind her, and nothing else mattered.

Her body lay exhausted on the ground. She tied the scarf around her head and burst into tears. The tears poured out, burning the corners of her swollen eyelids. They were absorbed by the dust sticking to her eyelashes. They flowed down her cheeks like black threads.

She moved her head towards the man. He was standing in his place. He had taken off his shirt and exposed his chest. With his fingers he began to play with clots of hair that were sticking together. There was something inhuman in his naked body. She could not place her head on this chest. A broad square locked like a box. The thought came to her to open it with the chisel. But her hand did not move from its place. The thought was a fantasy that used to come and go in her head.

She stretched out her hand to take hold of the chisel. At that moment a sharp pain ran through her side. As if a congealed piece of oil had entered her lung with the air.

She let out a cry and rushed to cling to his feet. She remained standing, hesitating a little, her features hanging limp. She had no hope that he could remove the pain. But he was there. There was something in his presence, or in the movement with which she rushed to his feet. Or in his features apart from their limpness, or in the startled look in his eyes. There was something there that lightened the pain.

She was able to move her feet a few steps towards him. Her hand was on her breast pressing on the pain. She approached him until there was no more than a step between them. She had never before in her life seen the face of a man in such despair.

She raised her eyes to heaven. The sun was setting and the light was fading. She suddenly found herself bending over as if she was going to sleep. Her neck bent forward at a sharp angle. The movement startled her and she came upright again. She took hold of the leather strap over her shoulder and pulled it strongly. The bag slipped off her shoulder and fell to the ground. The chisel fell out of it suddenly.

A fresh breeze arose. She opened the buttons of her cloak and felt the freshness on her bare skin. The wind had a refreshing feel to it, which brought back to her something of her childhood happiness. Not all her childhood had been filled with sadness. There were some moments of happiness. When she was sitting on the bridge at sunset. She saw him looking at her. He was staring at her bare chest. She had no desire to seduce him. All she wanted was the breeze. It refreshed her swollen skin and dried her sweat.

Her nakedness was natural under the pressure of the heat. But he continued to stare at her chest as if she had exposed it on purpose. She was about to reach out her hand to close her cloak but she did not do so. She closed her eyes helplessly. Yes, she could flee. Had she not fled once before? Had she not made a hole in the wall and crept out to go on leave?

She looked around her. There were no four walls to hem her in. Just vast areas of liquid. A pond or a lake with black waves. She could find a boat or make herself a coracle of palm leaves. As a child she used to make little boats from the leaves of the date palm. She also used to make aeroplanes with wings of leaves.

She began to brace her body and to stand up. She moved her feet in the other direction, away from the man.

She moved away a few paces. When she looked at him from

some distance away, he seemed more human. He looked at her more tenderly. Her eyes were drawn towards him. He could call her if he wanted. But he was silent, and in his silence there was something devious.

She went no more than a few steps and then she came back. The man had gone inside the house. She saw him lying on his back, letting water drip into his mouth from a bottle. With the edge of his lower lip he wiped away a drop that had fallen on his upper lip. He looked around as if he was not expecting her to come.

'You are selfish, aren't you?'

'Yes, but I'm better than many other men.'

'That's certain.'

'Tomorrow I will give you your portion, when they pay the grant.'

'Tomorrow I won't be here.'

'What are you saying?'

'I beg you. Help me go back. My husband is waiting for me. He may be assailed with suspicions, and my boss at work must have no fewer suspicions than he. I went on leave, and that is something that arouses suspicions. But I'm not interested in anything apart from searching for goddesses. Perhaps you have heard of the goddess Sekhmet.'

'Sakhmutt?'

He pursed his lips as he said the word. His bottom lip turned outwards and he changed the pronunciation of the 't' by velarising it.

'Don't you know anything about archaeology?'

'On His Majesty's birthday they order us to spend lavishly.'

'Spend what?'

'Bottles.'

'I don't want anything any more.'

'What's the problem then?'

'I don't understand why you don't set me free.'

'Set you free?'

'Yes. I am a human being like you, and I have rights.'

'What?'

'Women's rights! Don't you know about them?'

'We have never heard of anything like that. We have the rights of men only.'

She lowered her eyes and sighed silently. Her face dropped and her shoulders slumped. She didn't attempt to reply. It appeared that words were without meaning.

He also sank into a long silence. He lowered his head as if he was looking at his feet. Or perhaps he had fallen asleep. Then he raised his head, his eyes looking at her. 'Why don't you want to stay here?'

'Why do you want me to stay here?'

'My work is here.'

'Do you call this chore work?'

'There is a long queue of people waiting impatiently for my place to fall vacant.'

He raised his arm and pointed to a black line on the horizon. Her eyes followed the movement of his finger. The line was like a tilted disk, disappearing behind a dark cloud, which was dispersed a little by the light of the sun. The line appeared to move, like black particles, thousands of particles, appearing like heads stuck together, tilted downwards, moving forward slowly as if they were on the march. They advanced step by step with bent backs. Men with twisted moustaches, faceless women with heads tied with scarves. The storm rose and a new cloud appeared. They disappeared completely from sight. There was no trace of them apart from that black line that appeared on the horizon like an arc.

She moved her eyes towards the man. He took an axe and began to beat the ground. He was filling the jars one after the other. His back was towards her. She crept away on tiptoe. She could distance herself little by little and run away. Perhaps she would succeed in running away before he turned towards her.

She noticed the loaf of bread on the wooden board and suddenly felt pangs of hunger. She took the bag off her shoulder and stretched out her arm. She took a nibble of bread between her teeth, then another, then another. The man saw her eating. 'How can you eat my food and then refuse to obey me?'

'Is it your food?'

'Of course.'

'I'm not eating of the sweat of your brow. I sweat as well, like you.'

'Like me?'

'Yes. For example, don't I carry the jar to the company each day?'

'The company!?'

The word rang strangely in her ears. A mysterious word. The company. What is it? Who are the partners in this company? To whom do they sell the jars? How much do they pay for them each day? Does the man take a wage? From the day she had come, she had received nothing. She had never held any money in her hands.

The world became blurred before her eyes. She moved her head towards the man. He began to beat the ground with the axe, blow after blow. A slow heavy movement. Then he threw the axe aside. He yawned. He wiped off the sweat with the sleeve of his *jallaba*. He filled the basket up to the brim. He raised it slowly with a ponderous movement, then emptied it into the jar. The jar cracked with a loud noise.

'It's not right for a woman to work for money.'

'Then why should she work?'

'For a greater goal.'

The words seemed logical. There was another goal to her life. For the sake of the greater goal, she could submit herself to a smaller goal. She felt at rest with this thought.

She raised the jar with one hand, and placed it on her head. The muscles of her neck bent under the load. But it steadied itself once more. The congealed oil was very sticky. It shook in the belly of the jar and from its mouth arose something like steam.

She moved on her way towards the company. Her shadow was reflected on the surface of the lake. With the jar on her head, she appeared like the goddess Hathur carrying the disk of the sun between her horns.

She tensed the muscles of her neck as if with pride. Heat emanated from the base of the jar like the sun. She moved with firm steps, without giving heed to anything.

From a distance the company appeared like a black stain on an expanse that was even blacker. A piece of land rising into the sky like a chimney. It threw out flames and black particles that appeared to be red under the sun.

Perhaps she had been born here and she didn't have another life. She twisted her neck with a sudden movement and the jar almost fell. She raised her arm and grasped it with a swift movement.

The company seemed more distant as she moved nearer to it. The sun disappeared and night began to creep over the land.

It laid itself down on the land suddenly, as if it was going to sleep.

Since her childhood she could not stand anything on her head. She took the jar off and carried it on her back. Perhaps this would be a better position. If the heat flowed into her back, all that there was there was bone. Heat on the head dissolved the brain.

'Is this why donkeys carry things on their backs and not on their heads?'

The thought astonished her. Her mind became more active. The donkey seemed to her to be more intelligent than women. She also realised why men refuse to carry things on their heads. She moved the jar to the lower part of her back and it became lighter. A refreshing wind slowly entered her chest. Her head was liberated from the weight and a new thought came to her. Her astonishment increased the more she developed the thought. Her body began to tremble. A wave of rebellion swept over her like a feverish tremor.

She wiped the sweat from her brow with her sleeve. She contemplated her life. What was it that incapacitated her? In her childhood what had she wanted to be? Her body collapsed in exhaustion. She wanted to be a prophetess like the Lady of Purity, with her ability to restore movement to paralysed legs and sight to sick eyes.

'A woman prophet!? We have never heard of this before!'

'She's inherited the madness from her aunt.'

'A demon's got hold of her and she's become stubborn.'

She closed her eyes and went off to sleep. She was resisting despair by falling asleep. Her mind regained some of its enthusiasm. Hope crept into her body like worms creep into the ground. She looked at the watch on her wrist. Time was passing and she was lying down. She jumped up on her feet. She stretched out her hand and took hold of the chisel.

The land was changing as the oil changed. The oil was changing with the movement of the sun and the wind. Her breathing rose and fell according to the degree of hope or despair in her breast, and to the pulsing of blood from her heart to her arms, from her arms to her chisel, from her chisel to the ground, and from the ground to the oil, the wind and the sun.

Everything began to rotate in wondrous harmony as if it was the law of the universe. If the oil changed, everything around her changed. Perhaps the power of the oil is beyond belief or of an unfamiliar type. Congealed oil is not like liquid oil, and oil sludge that settles on the bottom has another consistency, and a completely different viscosity. In the bowels of the earth, everything changes, even humidity. And in her head thought after thought went round, and the chisel hit the ground blow after blow, without purpose. Nothing leaves any mark, and everything ends in nothing.

When she returned she saw the man lying on his back with his eyes open and a cigarette lit. He moved his head towards her a little and asked, 'Did you say something? Weren't you speaking?' He was gazing at the flame in his hand. Perhaps fire was salvation.

'What did you say?'

'Nothing.'

She said 'nothing' with a ring of submission. The place was bathed in silence. If one particle catches fire, fire will catch hold of everything. The thought of dying by burning did not attract her. She moved her feet towards the door. She held the knob with both hands. It would not open. It was permeated with damp and its bottom edge had stuck to the ground.

The man put out the cigarette against the heel of his shoe. Then he picked up the newspaper and hid behind it. She saw the picture of His Majesty and the banner headline:

ON THE OCCASION OF HIS BIRTHDAY, HIS MAJESTY ORDERS THE STATUE OF VICTORY TO BE WASHED.

She closed her eyes, then opened them. She saw something moving like a snake. It raised its tail when it saw her, as if it was greeting her. She nodded her head to return the greeting. It exhaled air with an audible sound. She realised that it was saying something in another language. She nodded her head as a sign of understanding.

The snake changed into a sudden movement with her hand. She pulled the newspaper from over the head of the man.

'What is happening is unendurable by any human being, and you stretch out in your chair smoking and reading the newspaper as if there was nothing wrong with the world.'

'What's wrong?'

'This is wrong. Can't you see?'

His eyes followed her finger as it pointed up in a circular movement.

The Statue of Victory was made of alabaster covered with a black layer of oil particles. Before being washed its face looked black, covered with oil stains.

She could not fail to attend the celebrations. The order had been issued typed out and sealed with the sign of the falcon. The women must undertake the washing and the men must stand in ordered ranks, and salute.

She did not know how much time she spent washing the statue. It seemed to be submissive to her ministrations. She breathed in time with the movement of her arms, and the beating of her heart under her ribs, and the ticking of the watch on her wrist. The process of washing seemed endless, mindless perhaps, an attempt to escape from some other activity. After washing, the face became white in colour, like the face of His Majesty, plump, barrel-chested, with two prominent breasts like the face of the goddess Ekhnaton.

She continued to gaze at the statue for a long time. A wind arose from the south and filled her eyes with particles of oil. The pain increased until it burned and she closed her eyelids. From behind she heard the voice and the man's hand almost touched her.

She half-opened her eyes. He was not the man. She saw a woman standing, carrying on her head the planet Earth or the disk of the sun. She had two long horns that curled forwards. The light was dim, or perhaps the swelling of her eyes had weakened her sight. She could not see the face of the woman. She could not be certain of what she carried on her head.

Her mind was no longer able to make sense of things. Everything blended together inside her head with the intense heat. Sweat fell in drops from her nose. Her arm was not strong enough for her to raise it and wipe the sweat. She left it to drip copiously with her tears. Perhaps the disk of the sun was the enemy. Her mind worked once more as she sprawled on the ground, but the voice of the woman interrupted her thoughts, 'Get up, sister, and have a bath. Many happy returns.'

She turned over in her place and considered her. Her *jallaba* was long and black. She had the features of her aunt. Her neck twisted under the load. Next to her was the washingbasin. She took a piece of rock and went to rub her cracked feet and to remove the layer of black. She polished her feet energetically as if they were the feet of the Statue of Victory. The rubbing brought on a pleasant stupor in her head. She did not know what was the relationship between feet and head.

If it wasn't for the beating of the sun, and some embarrassment, she could have taken more enjoyment in the process of washing. She was not related to her; she was not her aunt. She took off all her clothes. Nakedness was frightening. She had never previously had occasion to strip naked in front of a woman or a man, especially her husband. In his sight, she was as pure as the Virgin Mary. For his part, her boss at work used to call her the Lady of Purity. Until, that is, he suddenly began to search her.

'Where is the pamphlet?'

'What?'

'The pamphlet that you've concealed.'

'I haven't concealed anything.'

'I saw it on you, in your handwriting, against His Majesty.'

'I haven't written anything. 'Raise your arms!'

'She raised her arms high. She felt his fingers searching between her breasts. They dropped lower to the forbidden regions.'

This is violation of the sanctity of the body. 'When she regained consciousness, she was screaming.

Where were the rights of women? She found herself lying in bed. Around her were women carrying jars. Over their eyes was a cloud. A dark layer of oil covered the pupil and there was an order from His Majesty: 'Any woman detained with paper and pen in her possession shall be prosecuted.'

Whenever she looked into their eyes, the intensity of the pain increased. They disappeared one after the other. One of them went first and was followed by the others. She heard their voices through the wall. They were gasping with disjointed voices. The joints of their necks cracked under the jars. The beat of their feet on the ground was muffled. The wind carried it under the bridge where the houses of the village were. The barking of the dogs came from afar. The question turned over in her mind, 'Should she flee by herself or should she reveal her plan to them?'

★ ★ ★

The plan had not been revealed yet. And her boss at work had written a secret report. The reports about her were only written in secret. Another woman had taken her place in the department. You would see her sitting in her office looking around her in curiosity. She would not stop looking until she knew the secret. She opened her drawers and searched through her papers. She latched on to an old love letter. Some verses of poetry that she read repeatedly. Between every verse her breathing would rise in a long sigh. In the secret dossier she came across her date of birth, and a picture of her aunt with a scarf around her head. Her eyes would rest on the house. A room without a toilet in the alley. Curiosity pushed her to look through the crack in the door. She saw the room lying in darkness, bare of furniture. She would cast a sideward glance at her husband sitting reading the newspaper. He would move his head a little and you could see his nose from the side. Big and beak-like, it resembled His Majesty's. But his picture was not published and his name was unknown. Sitting motionless and completely silent. The silence betrayed her absence. Her soul was full of envy because she had been able to flee. How had she fled? She had gone on leave and not returned, had she? She nursed the secret in her heart and then it burst out in spite of her. The rumour spread through the archaeology department. Male and female colleagues whispered together and a look indicating jealousy would float into their eyes.

This jealousy was not an irrational thing. It was totally natural in the eyes of the employees. For there is nobody more envious than the employee. Especially in the archaeology department. He sees people moving around him and he is imprisoned behind his wooden desk. People speak about the future and he lives in the past with his archaeological digs. Life passes him by. Nothing will change in the universe whether he lives or dies. There is nothing before him apart from the slumber that overcomes him as he reads the newspaper or searches for gods in the bowels of the earth. A type of divine love, which leads him to long for death, or to go on leave.

★ ★ ★

'Did you ever have a row?'

'Never,' replied her husband in the interrogation room. The policeman swung his body round in the chair.

'Do you think that she could have committed suicide?'

'Not at all.'

'Didn't she ever long for death?'

'Never.'

'How do you explain her disappearance then?'

'Nothing.'

'Nothing?'

'Yes, nothing.'

Her husband said 'Nothing' through pursed lips. He yawned until the bones of his jaws cracked. He turned his face towards the journalists. A camera flashed and burnt the surface of his eyes. His picture had appeared on the inside page. His jaw was square and his face was longer than it should be. There were no distinguishing features except a black mole above his left cheek. A smile escaped from between his clamped lips.

From his childhood he had imagined seeing his picture beside His Majesty's. His mother raised her arms to heaven beseeching the Lady of Purity that her son might become like the King. Why not, our Lady of Purity? Was he not born from a stomach like the one from which the King was born?

The panting of the women had disappeared along with their black shadows. Dogs began to bark in the distance. Dogs do not bark without reason. Are those women planning some move? There had been a look of rebellion in their eyes under the clouds of particles. A counteraction always on the point of being launched.

She opened her eyes and felt the burning of the sun. She was chattering deliriously. The word 'counteraction' drew around her clouds of fantasies. She saw herself ensconced like a jar on the heads of the women. They were carrying her along the alleys of the village. Their eyes were looking down on her from the roofs. They were kicking the ground with their feet and the picture of His Majesty was shaking at the top of the pillar, then it fell under their feet and they trampled on it.

She rubbed her eye with her fingertip. The pain was burning and she was stretched out on the ground, totally worn out. A fly flew by and settled on her nose. It began to nibble a bit of peeling skin. She raised her hand to brush it away, but the fly remained in its place. In her other hand the chisel was lying, motionless. Dogs were barking at each other in the distance, children were throwing stones at each other and men had their hands intertwined. Oil was gushing out in all directions and the colours of the sky were being swallowed up in the darkness.

'Prepare the supper!'

The man's voice pierced her ears. An imperative tone, completely natural when a man addresses his wife. An unpaid servant. Wasn't he her husband? She didn't know exactly when he had married her. Probably he had married her in her absence and the marriage contract had been prepared without her being present. The woman didn't attend her marriage ceremony anyway, and all the formalities could be completed without her existence.

The muscles of her fingers contracted around the chisel. A sudden surge of anger, which pumped the blood into the muscles. She raised her hand and struck the bowels of the earth. The head of the chisel hit something solid. A statue of bronze or alabaster, but its colour was less opaque, like volcanic glass.

Her fingers trembled as she pulled it out. Her fingertips caressed its soft surface. She fingered the neck and the chest. Her hand bumped into the prominent breasts. It was the goddess Hathur, bare-chested, holding her breasts in her palms in a position of total giving, holding a pair of snakes.

She would have seized hold of it had a sea of oil gushed out and submerged everything. Could it be Noah's flood? She had read about the flood in the book of archaeology, years of famine and drought, and advancing deserts and mountains. The earth was on the brink of the Ice Age and an imbalance had occurred in the vital balance of the atmosphere. The regime had been overthrown after the slaying of the mother goddess.

'Prepare the food! I'm hungry!'

She didn't hear this time. The sound of the gushing oil covered everything else. Her fingers relaxed around the chisel and fell back. The current would have snatched it from her if she had not stretched her torso as far as she could and peeped over the edge with her head. The swirling oil resembled a whirlpool. It rotated as swiftly as the earth rotates. Smoke rose from it as if it was boiling. She was dressed as a child crying, 'Mummy!'

Her body convulsed with the name 'Mummy!' For the first time she had said the name clearly. Since she was born, she had never called out for her mummy. That was probably because her mother had died giving birth to her, or because she had not yet learnt how to speak.

When the storm died down, she stretched out languorously. She was gasping and her eyes were closed tightly. The picture of the ancient flood returned to her. Fear of drowning filled people's hearts. At the height of their fear, they became eagerly attached to the name 'Mother'. When her aunt was frightened, she used to cry out 'Mother' instead of 'Mummy'. She spat into the opening of her *jallaba*. The alleys were narrow and blocked with piles of dung. The houses were made of mud and were totally invisible apart from little lamps that drew shadows like ghosts. The village night was frightening, a haunted night, in which it was quite appropriate for Satan to make his rounds. Her aunt was walking under the bridge when she saw him that night. He was Satan in flesh and blood having taken on human form. And people said, 'The flood is from Satan.' And they began to call on the mother goddess to save them,

Our beloved mother, where are you?
Has Satan eclipsed you?
Has he placed a thick veil over your face?
Has he distorted your image and changed your name?

She had been sleeping when her aunt read her the song in the book. The sound of their singing seeped into her ears under the pillow. The singing was interrupted suddenly and her husband's voice rang out, 'I'm hungry. Can't you hear?'

She didn't change the position of her body, which was stretched out over the edge. His angry voice came from afar, as if from the bottom of the well. She could scarcely hear it with her ears. The voice only touched the edge of her consciousness. She turned over onto her other side in order to reduce the intensity of the sun. In spite of the anger, his voice resembled that of a suckling child. Hadn't his mother weaned him yet? Before her aunt weaned her, she used to clutch the teat. It was dark, the heat had decreased somewhat after the sun had set, and the sound of the flood was like the waves of the sea.

'I'm hungry.' His voice had become full of gentleness. Hunger refines men's nature. It reveals the man under the rough exterior. Her heart was filled with a mother's compassion. She went into the kitchen and lit the stove. She pressed on the revolver and a spark shot out. She laughed like she used to do when she was a child. She heated the soup in an aluminium saucepan. She peeled the potatoes and cut off the heads of the onions with a knife. Steam rose from the saucepan. Particles of oil dropped from the ceiling. They formed a dark layer on the surface of the soup. She went and fished them out with the handle of the ladle. However, the particles kept on falling and she had to keep on fishing them out, until finally she succeeded in getting them all out, apart from a few black particles which kept floating on the surface like flies on a corpse.

He sipped the soup with a sound like pipes sucking up oil. Between every sip he would rage with a sound like the roar of the wind. After he finished his food, silence fell. He closed his eyes without taking off the company uniform. It was blue in colour, but covered with oil stains. It exuded the smell of the gas that was stored in the bowels of the earth. Sleeping, he looked like the baby girl she had given birth to in her previous life, but who had subsequently died. When he woke up, she would take his clothes off, rub his body with a piece of rock, and then dry him with an old *sarwal*. She would twist the *sarwal* between her hands until it became like a bundle of aluminium wire. She dried him vigorously as if he was the bottom of a saucepan. In the distance dogs barked at each other and women gasped in unison. She shook her head in tune with them, her arms waving, her lungs rising and falling and her heart beating under her ribs. Then the movements became slow, monotonous and repetitious, sending her to sleep even as she stood there.

He yawned with a loud voice. She saw him smoking as he sat behind the newspaper. He would puff out the smoke between his lips and go off into raptures.

'Give me a puff too please!'

'What are you saying?'

'One puff of your cigarette.'

'Women do not smoke, by order of His Majesty.'

She clamped her lips shut and did not reply. She had fed him and washed him. She had treated him like her absent child. She had wiped away his pain. Didn't she have the right to go into raptures like him?

When he handed her the jar to carry it, she had a desire to pour it over his head. But she had second thoughts. She could obey him today for the sake of a higher goal tomorrow. She could not lose everything for one puff.

Smoke was escaping from his nostrils. The nostrils dilated and the little hairs inside them trembled with the intensity of the rapture. She inhaled one or two deep breaths of the air, and some smoke found its way into her chest. She puffed it out from her mouth and nose. Yes indeed, if life held no rapturous pleasure for her, she at least had a right to take a puff of the smoke in the air. Anger seeped out of her body with the smoke, and the world appeared less depressing, or rather, perhaps, the smoke had gone to her head and she felt she had come across some genius idea that would deliver her from her present life.

She had seen pictures of geniuses in the book. Clouds of smoke surrounded their heads. One of them had his head tilted sideways, leaning his chin on his hands. His eyes were half open, gazing upwards into space. The smoke rose from his dilated nostrils. In the book she also used to see pictures of the prophets. They too could only see God from behind a cloud of smoke.

She drew a deeper breath. Her head filled with smoke. Her mind seemed to pulsate under her skull, and she felt the idea being born. She encircled her head with her hands, afraid that the idea would escape her. The idea might creep out through the holes that opened onto her ears, eyes and nose. She pressed her hands on her skull, but she could not continue long and eventually let her arms fall by her sides.

'Are you sleeping on your feet?' She stretched and yawned with a sound resembling the bleating of a goat. She heard the voice, like the whistle of the wind. The storm roared and black particles crept under her clothes, invading the orifices of her body. She closed her eyes completely and wakefulness dissolved in a strange dream. She saw herself riding on the back of the chisel as if it was a horse. It galloped with her over an unknown city. Its buildings were tall, the tops piercing the clouds. Its streets were so narrow that there was only just enough room to pass. The chisel flew with her through the air without wings. It hovered above the roofs and she waved her feet as if she was playing on a swing. The women gazed at her with pleasure mixed with envy. Their hands were raised in the air clapping. Then the hands tried to drag her down, hoping to make her fall. She shook her legs vigorously so that the horse could climb with her again. By now the horse was no longer a horse but a palm frond that she rode on like the village children did.

Hands seized her and she fell. Her body plunged downwards and sank into the fog. Then she saw herself walking on asphalt that melted under her feet because of the extreme heat. A bit of tar stuck to the heel of her shoe, smelling of oil. She quickened her pace, panting, and went into a black building without windows or doors, but with iron pillars. A choking smell filled the building. The chisel was in her bag and she held on firmly to the strap over her shoulder. Her legs climbed the steps, almost slipping. She regained her balance without grasping hold of anything. There were no railings and the staircase was a narrow spiral one, which was not wide enough to permit her body to pass. She was pushed into a narrow door, which opened suddenly, and there she was inside the room, which was bare of furniture apart from a swivel chair and a worktable around which a number of men were sitting. All that was visible of them were their prominent facial features, the foreheads, the cheeks, the jawbones, the noses and the chins.

They did not raise their heads when she entered. They were standing over a book, their minds absorbed. They turned over the pages with knuckly fingers. They began from the cover and continued to the last page. Then they began again. 'Is this your name?'

The voice sounded like that of her husband, but the black pipe in his mouth indicated that it was her boss from work. He swivelled round, sitting in the chair. He came and stood directly in front of her. She saw his face and realised that he was the police interrogator. Silence fell. She heard the rustle of papers, and a cloud of smoke rose to the ceiling. His finger pointed to the name on the cover of the book. 'This is your name, isn't it?'

'Yes.'

'And the book!?'

'It's about goddesses.'

'Isn't that blasphemy against the gods?'

She wanted to raise her hand and ask 'What is blasphemy?' and 'Where is the blasphemy?' But the fog prevented her from seeing. She heard a noise like an explosion coming from papers being torn. Her nose filled with the smell of smoke. The papers were burning. A spark had flown from the mouth of the burning pipe. The fire spread to the jars of oil. They exploded one after another and tongues of flame shot into the sky.

When she opened her eyes, her nose was full of smoke. The man was sitting in his place gazing at her. He imagined that she had stolen a cigarette from his pocket while he was asleep. Before he slept, he used to count his cigarettes, and the coins in his inside pocket. He used to hide the bottle in a place that was unknown to her. But smoke engulfed the place. It had crept over the houses of the village like a black mist.

The newspapers appeared stating that the fire had come about because of the intervention of Satan. The people of the village raised their arms towards heaven, and stoned Satan. But heaven did not listen to their entreaties. Satan used to walk on the bridge. The women's eyes used to stare at him through the shutters. Their bodies trembled inside their black *jallabas*. They would tie black scarves around their heads. One of them tied her scarf more tightly, twisting it three times. She knotted it above her forehead so that it looked like the head of a snake. She twirled round and kicked the ground with her feet. 'Our Lady of Purity!' The voices of the ladies rose, and the beating of the drums, the cries of the children, the cracking of sticks in the hands of the men, the croaking of frogs in the pond, the barking of dogs which came from here and there, and the dust rising into the sky. The universe filled with a black fog, which gushed over the land like a waterfall. It was neither liquid nor smoke, and you could not catch hold of it with your fingers.

'Where have you hidden the bottle?' said she, waking up suddenly from sleep. Her throat was chapped with thirst and there was a burning fever in her stomach. The man was lying down with his face to the wall. She slipped her hand under his head. All there was there was the stub of a burnt cigarette. She crept away on tiptoe. She opened the door and went out. The wind no longer felt like wind. When she stretched out her hand in front of her, it bumped into something solid. She retreated step by step until she re-entered the door backwards. It was a movement that her body had not been accustomed to perform since childhood. She used to walk forward with her face looking backwards, or go out of the door backwards. Her aunt would be standing in front of her, gazing at her with eyes that made her body tremble. And all because she had asked her, 'Is it true, Auntie, that Satan walks on the bridge?'

Her eyes would dilate. The storm was at its worst. The rain was pelting down and all the lights had been extinguished. All she could hear was the whistle of the wind. Her aunt's voice resonated in the darkness of the night, 'The only devils are the children of men.'

Before dawn she heard the dogs barking, and the creaking of wheels combined with the whistling of the wind. The men pounced on her aunt and carried her to the cart. She jumped up and ran behind them. She stretched out her arm as far as it would go in order to hold her hand. Her legs sank up to the knees in the lake. The wheels cut through the black water and disappeared in the darkness. The dogs swam behind it. All that was visible of them were their oblong heads like a swarm of frogs. She plunged into the lake. Her ears filled with black mud and voices came from the bowels of the earth, 'A woman who does not believe in the existence of Satan ... She is mad, Your Majesty ... An unbeliever ... Yes, Your Majesty, unbelief and madness are the same thing.'

By that time she was completely submerged. All that was visible of her in the twilight was an outstretched arm, all five fingers contracted, clinging on to a piece of congealed mud.

Arms stretched out to her to pull her out. As they had pulled her out of the womb. Women's faces surrounded her, brown and wizened. The wind pushed in to her chest with a high-pitched noise like a cry and she opened her eyelids, which had stuck together. She saw the man stretched out with eyes closed, his arm gushing with blood. She was by his side, naked, and the colour of the blood was black. Some drops of the blood had congealed while others remained gelatinous. She stretched out her arm to take hold of the railing. There was a strange smell, like gas gone bad.

'Get the tea ready!'

She heard his voice as he pulled up his *sarwal*. His upper half was naked. He was sitting in front of the doorway of the house. Around him were four men. They were all absorbed in some game or other. Thick square cards. He was sitting in the middle, dealing the cards to them. His body was at ease on the seat. The place of honour suited his body completely, and harmonised with his features. His fingers gathered the cards, then spread them out and then gathered them again. The eyes of the others were fixed eagerly on his hand.

'Tea!'

His voice had a commanding tone. As if he were her husband. She looked at him through a veil. Perhaps they had exchanged her husband for another man. The cards rustled as they were dealt. The men's faces were tense. Their eyes were fixed on the cards. Inside each eye the pupil swivelled. They had to be five not four. The head of the fifth was hidden behind the newspaper. Was he her husband? His legs were stretched out in front of him. His feet were large and his toes were stuck together by a black membrane between each toe.

The sun had begun to fall below the horizon. A pale light fell on the first page. Black particles swam in the slanting rays. At the top of the page she read the date: Tuesday the 16th. She looked at her watch. It was two o'clock and the minute hand was moving. Of course, time was passing as usual. She read the big banner headline:

HIS MAJESTY DECLARES WAR ON SATAN.

The playing cards were not ordinary ones. Rather they were something like chess pieces. The bodies of the pawns were made of wood, standing in their places unable to move. Big fingers enclosed them and moved them from place to place.

'Check!'

It was definitely not her husband's voice. He was no longer asking for tea. He was absorbed in the game. It appeared that the king did not want to be in check. He raised his voice repeatedly. 'Check!' His tone began to be dominated by anger, and uproar ensued.

'These are the rules of the game, brother!'

'You're cheating!'

'I'm more truthful than you are!'

'You're ignorant!'

'You're as thick as a donkey!'

They left the king and became involved in hand to hand fighting. Dust rose in the air, the drizzle of their saliva was sprayed all around, and they began to pant. None of them paid attention to the newspaper. The wind rolled it away, turning over page after page. Suddenly she saw a picture that looked like her: 'A woman went on leave and did not return. She must be found dead or alive. It is forbidden to give her shelter or protection.'

She did not have the nose they showed in the picture. Could it be the nose of another woman who went on leave? Her boss at work said that she had a Roman nose. At first she imagined that he was teasing her somehow. In her eyes, the Romans were meat eaters.

On the same page she saw the picture of the interrogator. He was sitting swivelling his chair. His back came to the wall and his face was towards her husband.

'Is this your wife's picture?'

'Yes.'

'Are you sure?'

'Yes, I'm sure.'

'A hundred per cent?'

'Nothing is a hundred per cent sure.'

'Then you're not sure.'

'Yes and no.'

'What do you mean by yes and no? Is that an answer?'

'What is the answer?'

'Either yes or no.'

'Then yes.'

'Then you're not sure.'

'Yes.'

'A hundred per cent?'

'No.'

The policeman beat the ground with his feet, and the chair swivelled round without stopping. Her husband seized the opportunity to hide his face behind the newspaper. When the chair stopped swivelling, the interrogator was facing the wall. He began typing, then swivelled round. Her boss at work was also sitting there, with his black pipe quivering between his lips, smoke rising from it.

'I'm not going to extol her nose, for I'm not impressed by Roman noses. I prefer national noses of the snub-nosed type.'

'What are you saying?'

'She was always an obedient woman, and there was nothing in her to arouse desire.'

The interrogator was swivelling his chair. The stormy wind was turning over the pages. There was no proof of anything. The newspaper was open before her eyes. Her picture appeared and then disappeared with the movement of the wind. News about lost persons was lower down on the page. It was natural for people to disappear. There was a law concerning men who did. The woman had to wait for her lost husband for seven years, and not take another man. The embryo remains alive in

the womb seven years, and it remains the property of the lost man until he returns. The woman is no more than a container. Lost women have no law concerning them. A woman does not have to be lost in order for her husband to take another woman.

She closed her eyes in the face of the wind. The rays of the sun were like a flame. The idea revolved in her head, as painful as a nail. If the interrogation was continuing, then no doubt there were campaigns to find her, and people tracking her down. Perhaps there were pedigree dogs – that imported type that distinguishes the smell of human beings. They train them to pick up the smell from far away, to see stars at midday, to type on typewriters and to use modern instruments. She did not know anything about modernity. All she knew about it was related to the past and to archaeology. The goddesses Hathur or Sekhmet would not protect her from any trained dog. But there were hidden depths to the matter. Perhaps it was due to that other man. Could he have sent the information about her to the police? Or perhaps it was her boss at work? He had hinted covertly at the shape of her nose. This was a clear invitation to her relating to something more than her nose.

She woke up to the sound of regular snoring. The man was sound asleep in the doorway. He was breathing loudly as usual. He was inhaling the air, his lips quivering. He was lying on his back with his right calf over his left, shaking his foot in the air. The sun had risen to its zenith. The heat had reached that temperature that destroys everything, even the last remaining vestiges of shame. She saw him pull his *sarwal* off as well. He became naked as the day he was born. But shame quickly returned to him when the sun set, so he put on his *sarwal* while his upper half remained naked.

Her eyes were not following the movement of the sun. His gaze was fixed on the picture in the newspaper. Under the Roman nose, her mouth was clamped shut. One corner of each eye was swollen, and her full name was missing. There was no police report. Perhaps the man had stopped sending information.

The relaxation she experienced diffused a sort of energy through her body. She jumped up from her place and stamped on the congealed oil. She was only wearing a baggy *sarwal*, which billowed up around her. Her torso was totally bare. The wind, little though it was, somehow found its way under her armpits. She raised her arms upwards, conscious of a certain repose. The oil had piled up around her waist where it held the strap firm. She wanted to scratch the corner of both her eyes, when suddenly she remembered the thirst that burnt her stomach.

She turned round to look for the bottle. As she turned the sun shone directly into her eyes. She could not take a step towards the house. The world around her appeared to burn with a red flame. There was no sign of the man. That was natural, for he used to disappear when he wished, and return when he wished. He could absent himself for seven years, and she would have to wait for him, by order of the law.

The disappearance of the man appeared normal. With the flood of oil, it was possible for anything to vanish in the twinkling of an eye. Immediately outside the doorway, the waterfall was gushing as if the storm was beginning once more.

When she went to cross over the threshold, she saw the chisel lying there. Around its head, the strap was wrapped in a knot. There arose in her body a feeling of familiarity. As if she was seeing the absent man, who had returned disguised as a chisel.

Perhaps something had happened. The iron chisel began to have a human aura, which dispersed the gloom. She stretched out her hand to it, and cuddled it at her breast. Like a mother finding her lost child. As if the chisel was moving by itself. She slipped to the ground, digging with its little pointed head with an amazing determination. It kept digging with a stubborn determination. As if it was a child looking for its mother and knowing for certain that she was there, lying in that hole in the bowels of the earth.

'Won't you ever stop looking?'

His voice startled her. She froze in her position. The chisel fell from her hand. The blue veins stood out on her chapped hands. She realised as he looked at her that her breasts were bare. She enclosed her chest with the bed sheet, her eyes half asleep. She was not properly awake and she did not know if he was her husband or a stranger. If he were her husband, it would be better if she screamed. For she did not remember that she had married a man with this appearance. If the man were a stranger he would pass on his way without any need for her to scream.

When she screamed, her voice was alien to the world of men. She probably did not open her mouth for fear that it would be filled with particles of oil. Nevertheless, she saw the women gathering around her, with jars on their heads. She realised that she was under observation, that their ears could hear her voice even if it had not emerged from her mouth, and that their eyes were staring at her with a sort of anger.

'You're a woman like us. Why don't you carry a jar?'

She wanted to prove that she was not like them and that she could not live and die like an animal. 'I have another goal.'

'What's that, sister?'

She remembered everything all at once. She began to tell story after story. She began with her aunt, and Lady Zaynab, and the Virgin Mary, and that she wanted to be a prophetess so that she could heal people from illnesses like the goddess Sekhmet.

The name Sekhmet rang in the air, which was swimming with particles of oil. The 't' became velarised and the women no sooner heard the name than they tied their black scarves around their heads and began to strike their cheeks and cry all together, 'Sakhmutt!'

It is not strange that everything was turning out like this. It was as if she had returned to her childhood, when her aunt used to tie a scarf around her head, and pour invective on anybody who came near her. If the women of this village were like her aunt, then the black flood would inevitably be considered a natural event. Her heart filled with despair and her eyes darted around looking for a way out.

She saw one of the neighbour women carrying a jar on her head. Her face was completely hidden behind a heavy black veil, and all she could see of it was half an eye, and something like a volcano exploded inside her, 'You're not a blind ox going round and round driving a water wheel. You must have the right to see what's around you, mustn't you? Or have you committed a crime in secret so that you're no longer able to appear among the people of the village with your face uncovered?'

'I don't want to uncover my face.'

'Is there a reason why you conceal yourself so much?'

'There's no reason why I should uncover my face.'

'You could at least see the world.'

'See what?'

'The world. Isn't it sufficient to see the world? Don't you feel a desire to see the world around you?'

'I used to have such a desire, then I became weary with everything.'

'Listen, sister! Even the ox tears the bandage off its eyes, and animals in cages kick.'

'I used to kick a great deal until I became weary with kicking as well.'

The neighbour suddenly changed her tone and said tenderly, 'We heard you crying. Was he beating you?'

'Beating me?'

Astonishment showed in her question. Was the man beating her with the head of the chisel? Anger overwhelmed her. She didn't want anybody to know. But it appeared that nothing was hidden in this village. The surveillance was masterly. She wanted to hide her face. Would she never confess that he had been beating her? What if the people of the village found out that she was like other women? A shudder ran through her body. Her skin was marked all over from the beatings. And the dryness in her throat. She wanted to let her body fall to the ground. But eyes were open around her, waiting for her to fall, and if she fell once, anybody could do anything to her. It was better for her to confess. She was not capable of fleeing.

The man had returned. She saw him approaching her from behind. He pressed his right knee in her back, then enclosed her with one arm. A smell of stagnant oil came from under his armpit. He passed his chapped fingers up and down her spine. She remained transfixed in her place, then she called out in pain when he pressed roughly on the last section of her spine.

'Do you feel any pleasure?'

'No.'

The man laughed and it appeared that he was caressing her in preparation for something. Although his movement was sudden, it appeared natural, or perhaps as if his fingers had slipped by themselves in an innocent way.

She turned round to confront him. There was no innocence, and there was no instinct for sexual love. He was pushing her to kneel, and after she had knelt down, anything would become possible. She saw that sleep was her one refuge. Perhaps she was in fact sleeping, because her breathing was loud. Her calves and her arms were trembling. Was she angry? Perhaps, because this man was always trying to spoil her sleep, and he succeeded in doing so whenever he pleased. By contrast, he was able to go off into a sound sleep without anything disturbing him.

When she turned over in her sleep, particles of oil stuck to her cheeks. Around her eyes, a particle would stick in a corner and she would wipe it away with a fingertip. She stretched a hand out in the darkness looking for the bottle. It was not there. The man was lying with his face to the wall and his back to her. His back appeared less well banqueted than his face. The matter came within the realms of possibility. But the night was long, and did not want to end, and sleeplessness like a hammer was beating in her head. She tied her scarf and fastened it above her forehead as she used to see her aunt doing. She closed her eyes and gained control of her breathing. She bent her knees and curled up in a ball like a foetus. She tried to remember the face of her mother before she gave birth to her. She followed the path that she walked along every day from the house to the school. There was a tree and a long river. She saw her usual place on the bridge where she used to sit at sunset, waiting for the lights to appear. She began to recite the names of the stars. She began with Saturn and Jupiter and ended with Venus and the whole galaxy. She tried to count on her fingers the names of the ancient goddesses, beginning with Nun and Namu and ending with Nut and Sekhmet.

However, sleeplessness did not leave her. It continued to beat her head like a hammer. She moved her eyes towards the man. She saw him covering his face with the newspaper. He was still sleeping or perhaps he had been reading and then gone to sleep while he was reading. His breathing was regular, like snoring. The rustling of papers at the mercy of the wind. Dogs barking from afar and women gasping, their necks cracking under the jars. However, the roar of the gushing waterfall overwhelmed all other sounds. Sleeplessness like a hammer beat her head, and the watch on her wrist ticked, and the pounding of her heart under her ribs, and her breathing, all these sounds beat in her ears.

She clamped her eyelids closed in a last attempt to sleep. However, she had no sooner closed her eyes than she fell into something like a well. All sound stopped. Time froze. The watch on her wrist no longer made its ticking sound. Particles of oil crept under the watch face and covered the hands. The second hand also stopped moving. Nothing moved apart from the pages of the newspaper that moved by themselves at the mercy of the wind. Each page revealed headlines in black and red script.

★ ★ ★

HIS MAJESTY DONATES THREE MILLION DOLLARS TO ZOO IN THE NORTH.

HALF A MILLION KILLED IN OIL WAR.

HIS MAJESTY FORBIDS THE DISTRIBUTION OF SWEETS ON CHILDREN'S DAY.

WOMAN SHOT AT FOR WALKING IN THE STREET WITH HER FACE UNCOVERED.

FOREIGN MINISTRY TO BE SOLD AT AUCTION.

OIL MINISTER RECEIVES A BRIBE LARGER THAN THE DEFENCE BUDGET.

DRUGS SOLD DURING TERM TIME.

AIDS SPREADS AMONGST CHILDREN.

FROM ATHEISM TO FAITH; FROM DOUBT TO CERTAINTY, BY THE CHIEF OF RELIGIOUS CONSCIOUSNESS AND THE FORMER HEAD OF THE COMMUNIST PARTY.

THREE WOMEN DIE IN QUEUE IN FRONT OF BAKERY.

EIGHT MEN RAPE LITTLE GIRL IN SCHOOL.

WOMAN SLAUGHTERS HER CHILDREN ON MOTHERS' DAY, THEN COMMITS SUICIDE.

MISSING MAN RETURNS AFTER SEVEN YEARS AND DOES NOT FIND HIS WIFE.

SHE IS WANTED DEAD OR ALIVE. IT IS FORBIDDEN TO GIVE HER SHELTER OR PROTECTION.

NEW INFORMATION OBTAINED BY POLICE ABOUT THE MISSING WOMAN. SHE WAS PASSIONATE ABOUT SEARCHING FOR MUMMIES AS A FORM OF RECREATION.

* * *

Time passed as she gazed at the word 'recreation'. Sleep must have overcome her, because her brain had stopped working. She did not know the meaning of the word. The sun had begun to rise. Perhaps the man had gone to the company. There was no noise from the jar carriers. She stood up on tiptoe. She slipped her hand under the bed and took out her shoes. They were full to the brim with oil. She emptied them and beat them one against the other. She placed the chisel in the bag, along with the map. She put the strap over her shoulder and made off before any eye could notice her. She closed her eyelids as she ran, as if closing her eyes would conceal her from others' eyes.

Deliverance appeared imminent, and flight easier if she continued without seeing. However, a new idea came to her mind. She could hide her face completely from people's view, without anyone seeing her face. It was a woman's right to conceal her face completely without anybody pursuing her.

However, in her case the situation was different. She was a barefaced woman. The newspaper had published her picture and her full name and address. Her room also appeared in the picture, the wooden bed with its collapsing boards, the dilapidated lamp on the desk covered with dust, and an open book with the head of a mummy peering out, and a desk drawer with some coins in it. A savings account book without any money in it. Then there was that rope hanging from the ceiling, as if prepared to be put around someone's neck, dead flies sticking to it, and at the end of it a burnt-out light bulb. Then silence. Yes, the silence that whistles in one's ears like the wind, or the snoring that a man usually makes when he is in deep sleep.

* * *

He had been a model husband, giving her a very peaceful life, and there was every sign that he sincerely wanted the marriage to continue.

'There is nothing to arouse suspicion apart from this wretched mummy head! Do you know whose head this is?' said the policeman as he swivelled round in his chair, shaking his hand in the air, holding a long cane in his hand, with which he pointed to the desk.

'The lady Sphinx's.'

Her boss at work replied in a confident voice, emphasising

the expression' the lady Sphinx' with his jaws and his teeth. Then he puffed out the smoke towards the ceiling, the pipe between his lips. He gazed at the policeman out of the corner of his eye, and confirmed in a loud voice, 'Yes, the lady Sphinx's.'

'The lady Sphinx's? We've never heard of it before.'

'Not hearing about it doesn't mean that it doesn't exist.'

'Is she the Sphinx's wife?'

The policeman was no longer settled in the chair. He swivelled round in it with his cane in his hand. He raised his arm and almost let it fall on the lady Sphinx's head. However, her boss at work was settled in his chair. He puffed smoke out of his nostrils and mouth. Smoke also came out of his ears. The black pipe was twisted forward at a sharp angle. His neck was also twisted at the same angle. His eyes looked upwards, half open. He gazed at the policeman out of the corner of his eye. 'After the Sphinx had usurped the throne, he ordered that the breasts be removed from the statue, and that a beard be added.'

'A beard!?'

'Yes. A borrowed beard. Watch!'

The policeman stretched out his hand with the cane in it and searched through the hair of the beard that was hanging from the chin. Her boss at work seized the opportunity and began to display the extent of his knowledge about archaeology, 'The sculptors dedicated themselves to the service of the new god, and art changed with the change in regime. Even the shape of the eyes changed. The straight eyes with the straight lines became curly lines with a squint.'

'A squint. What do you mean?'

'For example, when your right eye looks at your wife and your left eye looks at another woman.'

'That is natural, isn't it?'

'At that time it was unnatural. The lips also changed so that the smile became a scowl, and the open hand became locked closed with the fingers holding a cane.'

The word 'cane' came out of his lips with the smoke of the pipe, and the policeman jumped up without reason, hiding the cane in his hand behind his back.

'What do you mean by all that?'

'The lady Sphinx became the Sphinx, the soft smooth skin became hairy, the flood invaded everything, agriculture died, and the river waters changed to a black liquid with a sharp taste like salt. The new god ordered that breasts be removed from statues and a penis be added.'

The policeman's fingers froze on the typewriter. He could not bring himself to type the word 'penis'. He spun round without swivelling the chair. The movement did not appear in the picture in the newspaper. However, she could see everything as she slept, her eyes half closed. In the dream, reality appeared clearer to her.

★ ★ ★

In the dream she was thinking of something to say to her husband. For conversation had broken down between them from the time it had begun. There was no way of attracting him to her except by hiding herself. She also needed to attract other men and women. She dropped in on them each day in the office, her lips on the verge of breaking out in a smile, which would have broken out were it not for the frown on the ladies' foreheads, or the face of His Majesty hanging above their heads, or the picture of the god Ekhnaton before the breasts had been removed, or the daughter of the lady Sphinx who had removed from her mother the borrowed beard and revealed that she was a woman, Maryat-Ra, daughter of Hachapsut.

She used to open the door every day and lean over her statue. The only daughter who came to know the face of her mother. She used to sit at her desk looking at the faces of the women. The colour of their skin was the yellow of dry clay. Their heads had been carved from limestone. The realisation plunged into the depths of her that she was one of them. She swallowed the bitter saliva that overflowed with self-hatred. However, His Majesty's birthday was approaching and lights were being hung everywhere. The sound of music and singing rang in her ears. The children were wearing new clothes. The birthday celebrations in the houses were not like they were in the streets. There was nothing in the houses apart from husbands hiding their faces behind newspapers. They wrapped their heads in clouds of smoke. The wives stood in the kitchen, boiling frozen chickens with plastic heads. Tins of sardines made of magnetised tin. After eating there was a pleasure ship that went out to sea and did not return. In the long queue the lady martyrs collapsed. And at the end of the feast there was the dilapidated bus that overturned with all those in it. Before the day had passed the mother would slaughter her children and then throw herself in the sea. But nobody wanted to commit an offence and everybody performed the rites. They drew on his face a sign of rejoicing. They drew it with a coloured pen on his chapped skin. On the feast many faces leant out from the buses. And on the swings, and at the official celebrations. The only thing that dispelled the joy was a woman's bare face.

★ ★ ★

'Do you think that she's committed an offence?'

'Of course, naturally.'

'What do you mean?'

'Regardless of whether they are bare-faced or not, women are naturally wicked. Their cunning is indeed great.'

The voice became indistinct. She did not know if it was her husband or her boss at work. The face was like those of all other men. Bare with protruding eyes. He looked like someone who had woken up suddenly from sleep. He always showed jealousy towards her with regard to other men. He could become jealous of a relationship springing up between them and between other beings, like reptiles for instance. There was an ancient and incomprehensible enmity between him and the lizard. He was of the secretive type, as is usual with husbands and bosses. He did not inform anybody of the emotions of his soul. Up until now, under interrogation by the policeman, when he began to confess for the first time, 'I am beset by doubt.'

'We haven't heard this from you before.'

'This festival for instance.'

'What about the festival?'

'It makes us believe that something exists, while it has no existence. For this reason I prefer to work in the oil company.'

'Oil?'

'Yes, it's a liquid without any solidity, but it induces greater tranquillity.'

'I don't understand you.'

'I can't express myself more precisely.'

'Do you mean that you are involved with the woman?'

'No, but when the gushing increases, you yourself become like the oil, and so anxiety concerning death is dispersed.'

'There's no doubt that you are convinced of what you say,

and I think you've convinced me. She went on leave, didn't she?'

'You did not need to be convinced by me.'

'Pardon?'

'I think that there is in her, as there is in other women, something resembling oil.'

★ ★ ★

She held her head between her hands. For the first time she was hearing his opinion of her in her absence. Her constant presence concealed the truth, and absence in itself had become a goal which might reveal the emotions of his soul. In a manner of speaking, they were taking revenge on each other. He was wearing another, thinner, cloak. Dialogue between them had always ended in silence. She would leave the house for work each day as if she was leaving the grip of one person to fall into the grip of another. The ceiling was one and the same, like a vault. She pulled herself out of one vault to then come under another vault. And noise resembled silence.

She had never in her life asked for leave. It was a leave that she had not told anybody about. But envy had appeared immediately in the eyes of the women. It concealed itself under a layer of blame. They were all keen to offend, and were fed up with virtue. However, a request for leave required a permit and an unprecedented boldness in love.

'Love?!'

Yes, her heart could have palpitated, for the matter was extremely simple. Love was not lacking between her and the man. It tied them with such force that they had a quarrel every day.

There was no dissolution of their presence together under one roof.

'How was the relationship between the two of you?'

'Legal of course.'

'Was there a written contract?'

'Of course.'

'Of what type?'

'A contract of work and marriage.'

The policeman's eyes widened, and protruded even more. Then he swivelled in his chair, and his eyes dilated and came to rest on the ceiling.

'Do you mean that she was working in your home?'

'We all do that, don't we?'

'But we pay something at least.'

'To our wives?'

'To our lovers at least, isn't that the case?'

She had no desire to follow the rest of the interrogation. It became clear to her that flight was a sort of impossibility. She moved her feet over the ground, but did not progress a single step. The oil had soaked up her strength, and the man had finished filling the jar. He stood waiting for her to move. He began to stare at her for a long time and then raised his arm upwards.

She had the idea of resisting, of returning blow for blow. But her arm remained stuck to her side. Perhaps it belonged to a wife of oil that made things stick together. Or perhaps it was because the movement of his arm came suddenly and she did not have time to move. In the depths of her, she wanted to pounce on him. No part of her body moved except for her jaws. A cry came out of her throat.

'Don't cry out!'

'Are you hitting me?'

'All you have to do is to carry the jar.'

Her posture showed complete submission. She showed no resistance whatsoever. She was in an almost soporific state. Or perhaps the unexpected blow had deprived her of her will and made her kneel down like a camel. He placed the vase on her head and the jar on top. It was up to her to walk with the ladies to the company. Each one of them gave her a word, just for the sake of chattering on the way to the company.

'Do you understand? He will not beat you if you continue to work.'

'Did you disobey, sister?'

'It is not necessary for disobedience to happen. It is sufficient for you to think about it.'

'Sometimes the thought is more dangerous.'

She continued to move, her neck bent and her breathing coming in gasps. Her chest contracted, rising and falling with the movement of her breathing. With her tightly closed mouth she pushed out the particles of oil that flew around her, blowing them far away from her face. Her feet were stuck to the ground, sinking in below the knees. She let herself sink. There was nothing for her to do except to sink, to sink to the bottom. Once she had reached the bottom, the only way left would be up.

'Since I came I have not taken a wage.'

'Isn't it sufficient for you that I've taken you under my protection?'

She listened carefully to the expression 'taken you under my protection'. Her swollen eyes widened. Her aim was not to conceal herself. She had another goal. She definitely had one, even if she did not know what it was. Her feet moved without rising even an inch above the ground. There was not enough air for a deep breath. Her feet had swollen up and the skin was peeling off them. Oil crept under her nails like black mud. The jar on her head was heavy. Her brain heated up in the sun. Her lips were blue and open, and her breath came in gasps. She pressed with her teeth on her lower lip and blood burst from it. Its colour was blue, flowing hot down her chin. It had a sharp flavour on the tip of her tongue. She saw her picture reflected on the surface of the lake, like a ghost wandering over the face of the earth. She imagined that she cried, 'Help!'

She moved her neck towards the man. He could no longer hear her. Or if he heard her voice, he showed no sign of comprehension. He stared at her with a look that she had never seen before. Was he thinking of killing her?

She raised her arm and was about to throw the jar on his head. The move appeared to her completely legitimate. It was simply self-defence. Before her arm rose she looked in his eyes again and then stepped backwards. She had never before seen his eyes like this. The tremor was not apparent. Nothing in them expressed fear. But everything in him was as if scared to death.

She stretched out her hand and held his hand. Their fingers intertwined. He enfolded her with one arm, and she enfolded him with two arms. She closed her eyes and he closed his eyes. They moved along in each other's embrace, not seeing the ground beneath their feet. They sank together to the depths of the lake as if they were falling into the grip of a power that was greater than them, from which they could not free themselves.

At that moment they began to cling to each other's bodies. They held each other tightly. Their bodies became one mass, holding on to its parts, not wanting to be separated from any one of them.

'Was that love?'

Perhaps it was, because she had not heard a sound from the women. She had her eyes closed, lost in a sort of swoon. Then the voices of the women began to draw near her. Simply voices without bodies. She lent her head on the edge of the lake, as if she was about to take a drink of water or to disgorge something stuck in her throat. She heard her voice emerging from the depths of her as if she was vomiting. She reduced the pain in her chest and the lights began to appear. The queue was moving from afar along the skyline. Black ghosts with jars on their heads. The women approached her and their features became clearer.

'What are you doing here, sister?'

She saw the woman standing in front of her under a black her *abaya*, her body completely invisible.

'Me?'

'Yes, you? Who else would it be?'

'I am a researcher in the science of archaeology.'

A laugh rang out, followed by other faint suppressed laughs.

'Aren't you pregnant, sister?'

The word slapped her face like a blow. Pregnant? Could that be the reason for her detention here? She had been on strike against pregnancy from the moment her mother had died giving birth to her. She did not know what the point of pregnancy was. All women became pregnant.

'Would the whole world be turned upside down if one woman ceased being pregnant?'

'You stupid person!'

She was suddenly stripped of the darkness. Light appeared from afar. She stared in the direction of the woman, then bent down to sit on the ground. Under her bottom she discovered something hard. It was the chisel. Its head was wrapped with the strap from the bag, tied round its neck like a hangman's rope.

'Who among us is stupid?'

There was no sound. Just a silent murmur. Or particles in the air. She continued the conversation, beating the head of the chisel into the ground, 'Am I stupid? Is pregnancy all that concerns you? And me, what concerns me? Yes, I am a researcher. A researcher into what? Yes, I search for things that you don't know about. Numu the first goddess of the waters and Inana the mother goddess and Sekhmet.'

'Sakhmutt?'

'Isn't that an indication of your ignorance? It's better for you to leave me alone and carry your jar to the company. Women will remain in their state until the Day of Resurrection. Isn't there anybody to resist the oil? Don't you ever think of solidarity? Think about the matter. Don't blame anybody apart from yourself if you are buried in this lake. The oil will dominate everything, and it will make its way to every place. What has happened? Why don't you speak?'

Instead of replying, the woman hid in a way that seemed natural. She turned away without leaving any sound behind her, and there was no trace of her feet on the ground.

'Are you running away without a single word?'

She cried out in a high-pitched helpless voice, totally inaudible. She stopped moving and returned the chisel to the bag. He tongue began to rub against the roof of her throat. The sound of the rubbing was audible in her ears. She suddenly noticed the bottle on the shelf. It was totally dry. She raised it to her mouth and shook it a number of times. Not a single drop fell from it. She broke into sobbing, without making a noise, without tears and without sadness, despair, or anything.

She did not feel anything at all. It was another woman sobbing, not her.

She stuck to the ground pretending to be dead. She curled up, hoping to be rescued. She moved her eyes a little towards the door. The man was standing in the doorway, hair dishevelled. Had he been listening to her? She let her tears fall before she lost the opportunity. But weeping was not effective. Her lips moved in a sort of indecision. Perhaps a smile was preferable. She did not feel any prick of conscience. She could smile in his face in spite of everything, were it not for her intense weariness and a sort of pins and needles, like paralysis, running through her lips.

His face was towards the wall and his back towards her. The smile appeared unnecessary. The jar was hot because of the sun. Her breathing was irregular like that of an ox in the process of dying. She bent her neck the other way to lighten the load. She opened her eyes for a moment against the sun. Then she closed them immediately with great firmness.

When she arrived at the company her face was like a grilled fish. Her cheekbones were charred. On her head under the bottom of the jar was a deep hole. At the end of her neck was a swelling that oozed a black liquid. Her *jallaba* was covered in stains and the smell rose with the sweat.

Her boss from work stared at her through the corners of his closed eyelids, 'You must put on a clean cloak and perfume under your armpits.'

'Yes ...'

'It's time for His Majesty to arrive, and we don't want to offend his nose, do we?'

The muscles of her tongue would not obey her enough for her to reply, and her voice came out brokenly, 'On the night ... of the festival ... the full moon ... appeared ...'

She remembered a song from her childhood. She used to sing it with the girls in school when the headmaster arrived. They would sing it together: 'The full moon has risen upon us, and behind it comes the wife of the headmaster wearing circles of light round her neck, her hands and her feet. After her come the women racing each other on dainty heels. Their faces are turned downwards towards the ground and their bottoms shake from behind.'

The full moon has risen upon us ...

She did not know why her neck bent and twisted inwards. It appeared as if she was bowing to offer a greeting, seeking to hide the swelling sticking out between the folds of her neck. She wiped her skin with the palm of her hand, getting rid of the black stains. Why did she feel all this disgrace?

She thought that she was the sacrifice for the festival, and that she had to hide the traces of blood after the slaughter. She could have faced disgrace, if it wasn't for the man. If it wasn't for him she could be saved, but what after she was saved?

A sudden question came to her and she did not know what she would do if she was destined to be saved. 'I will write my life story.'

She heard the man laugh with a sound like a cough. He was bent over the jar, filling it. The jar also convulsed with the noise. She heard the rumbling inside its full stomach and realised that the oil was laughing too.

'Are you seriously thinking of writing?'

'Well, outside work hours revelation could fall.'

'Revelation?'

'Yes, revelation can sometimes fall on a cowherd or an oil caterpillar.'

'This oil will get the better of any revelation even if it falls from heaven.'

'Perhaps the outcome will be different if the revelation comes from the bowels of the earth.'

'What do you mean, woman?'

Her mind was not capable of reply. It appeared that the conversation was without meaning. The fever in her head grew more intense and the pain in the back of her head was like the banging of a hammer. She tied the scarf tighter and fastened it above her forehead. She did not know from what hole in her head emerged the idea of writing.

Revelation descended without need for writing or reading. His Majesty raised his head upwards and revelation fell from the sky like rain. They poured it into jars and on the Festival they distributed it with the allowances. A man received a whole jar for himself and a woman half. A woman could not receive her portion for herself. Her husband or some other representative had to deputise for her.

'Self-deception doesn't benefit anybody. Moreover, such fantasies are pointless.'

'What do you mean?'

'Writing for instance is no more than a sort of fantasy. If His Majesty neither reads nor writes, and the prophets didn't either, then that means that they did not need writing or reading. Moreover, what is the difference between carrying a pen and carrying a jar? Speak! Don't be stupid!'

The woman bent her neck and did not reply. Silence was a very good thing. It pushed her to close her eyes in total despair. She raised the jar onto her head and rushed outside. On the other side of the lake, a new storm was coming up. There was nothing for her to do but to keep on the track until the end. The idea of uncovering their faces was still far beyond their comprehension. They had been carrying jars from before sunrise and had disappeared in the darkness.

She stretched her arm upwards and shook the jar violently. All that poured out of it was a congealed drop of oil. Her eyes looked heavenwards. She could see nothing. She moved her fingers towards her nose and a smell of stale gas arose from them.

'What would happen if her life continued in this way?'

Perhaps there was a plot being hatched. The company boss had a light skin and prattled on in a foreign language. The newspaper said that he was a big-hearted man. He exchanged jars with His Majesty as a sign of affection. Also in this archaeological region there were the remains of the dead, and excavations made holy by the ancient gods and some goddesses from the Stone Age that they sought.

'Yes, the holy things have changed with the rising of the storm.'

'Aren't there any excavations here in the bowels of the earth?'

'There's only oil, woman.'

'What's this?'

'An extra bottle on the Festival of His Majesty. Didn't I tell you that he is big-hearted, full of compassion, and does not forget his subjects? How would you feel about having a swig? Let's celebrate the Festival of His Majesty together.'

She twisted her tongue inside her throat and moved her feet in the air like a hobbled ox. This man was not her husband, nor a police commissioner. Why didn't he undo her fetters and let her return? She was a young woman in the prime of her life; she bore the title of 'researcher' and had a husband waiting for her.

'I will fill a glass for you.'

'Isn't drinking forbidden?'

'It's all right as long as we're by ourselves and nobody sees us, although we need to be a bit cautious. They have distributed these bottles among us, and that means that drinking is permitted on the evening of the Feast until the dawn cannon is fired. Are you still alive? I see you're not breathing. Take this glass and forget everything.'

'I will forget.'

'Is that a promise?'

She shook her head as a sign of assent. The night of the Festival appeared totally suitable for flight. After he had drunk his fill, the man would lose consciousness. All she had to do was buy a return ticket. She opened the bag to take out some money. There was nothing there. She turned out the lining and shook the bag. Not a single coin fell out.

'Where's the money?'

'What are you saying?'

'I work and I deserve a wage.'

'I'd like to ask you a little question, simply to satisfy my curiosity.'

'Yes.'

'Don't I provide you with everything, even love? Are you lacking anything? Come on, speak and don't deny it!'

'You are an exemplary man, that's true. But I work all day and part of the night. Who pays my wage?'

'Your wage is due from God.'

'God? What are you saying, man?'

'Don't you believe that God exists, woman?'

His voice had become angry and the tone threatening. She was demanding her wage and he was demanding that she have faith. She did not know, but the situation had been reversed. He had become the person in the right, and she no longer had any request to make. He had put her in the dock and had begun to circle around her ruffling his hair and roaring like a lion.

'The heart of a woman like you isn't filled with faith. You deserve nothing apart from fire and burning. Come on, speak and defend yourself.'

She was tongue-tied and unable to reply. She was just as much a believer as the man, and more so. Her heart was big, bigger than his. It was large enough to embrace a faith bigger than his faith, a faith that also included the ancient gods — and the goddesses. But what was the relation of gods with money? She was a woman who did her work without shirking. She carried a jar on her head in an official oil company. The work was hard, and it had become even harder when the storm rose. She could have avoided all this trouble. She beat her feet on the ground, crying, 'All this toil!'

'Why did you come then?'

She froze in her place without speaking. The reply was as clear as the noonday sun. She had come because she could not continue there. Yes, she had come to avoid greater toil. That was the sum of it.

'Is that the sum of it?'

'Yes, that is the sum of it.'

The matter appeared very simple. Her lips let out a deep sigh as if she was resting. Her head suddenly bent forward over her chest as if she was sleeping. However, the movement woke her up and she paid attention once more. Her head was heavy and the heat, along with the heaviness of the jar, was gushing over her from above. It was as if she was carrying the disc of the sun at midday, even though it was night and the man was lying beside her with his eyes open.

'Haven't you got a BA?'

'What do you mean?'

'This matter upsets His Majesty and the boss of the company of course.'

'Hasn't any woman here managed to obtain a BA?'

'There was one woman, of poor parents. Her whole family were thieves. They said that she was possessed by a demon, for demons follow poverty, and thieves follow demons. Nevertheless, she did not succeed in running away.'

'How was that?'

'The newspapers published her picture and they brought her back before she had gone beyond the fixed boundaries of religion.'

'Do you mean that not a single woman has run away?'

'And not a single man.'

Her body slumped even as she lay there. It was as if she was falling into an even deeper sleep. She curled up in a ball like an oil caterpillar. Her face turned the colour of the earth. She pressed her hand against her breast. Then she burst out, 'There's no pulse!'

The man sprang up from the bed. He began to knead her heart with his fingertips. She was overcome with astonishment but could not refuse. He was seizing the opportunity of the absence of a pulse to press on her chest with his finger. He passed his finger through the cleft between her breasts. There was a congealed layer of oil with a sweaty smell. She mumbled in a sort of embarrassment, 'I was intending to take a bath, but ...'

'There's no need for embarrassment, for I'm not a stranger.'

The moon was casting a pale light on the lake, a round stain of faint white above a stretch of gloomy black. The window panel was made of planks of wood with a stout bolt. On it were growing clumps of oil; the edges were turning green. The window was low and had cracks in it, through which the women's eyes were looking. Three or four were trying to stop themselves laughing. One of the ladies was talking to her neighbour in the adjoining house. She was telling her what her husband did with her in bed. She interrupted her talk with bursts of braying laughter and then burst into tears.

'You have been married for ten years and you haven't become pregnant yet!?'

'It's God's command.'

'Rather it's that cursed second wife. She's cast a spell on you.'

'Is it magic then? What a disaster!'

'You are more fortunate than me. Your husband has only one other wife, but mine has three others. No sooner has one's spell finished its work than another begins.'

'Nevertheless, you became pregnant, didn't you?'

Seeping through to her through the wall, her voice sounded like her aunt's. She used to wrap a black veil around her head and go out. She used to wander through the alleys collecting seashells, and the bones of the dead from the bowels of the earth. She used to crush them in a grinder with alum and frankincense. She used to drink the potion before breakfast and before going to bed at night. She used to dampen her husband's pillow with it and the member between his thighs. Every demon used to have a special veil. It used to be written on by a blind sheikh in a darkened room. A blind man was more powerful than a sighted person in driving out demons. And of course a dead sheikh was more powerful than a blind one. The woman used to pay a piece of silver or a slaughtered chicken. A woman could not become pregnant without paying something.

The women's voices ended at night's end, when morning dawned with crimson rays which burned like tongues of fire.

'I beg you, haven't I got the right to have a drink of water?'

He must have been fast asleep. She did not hear a reply. His *jallaba* was torn from the chest. He was soaked in black sweat like congealed blood. Particles of oil stuck to his hair, and his lips were cracked like drought-stricken earth.

'Can't you hear me? A drop of water, please.'

Her voice was dry, and her body was trembling with fever. Heat was rising from under her skin, dissolving the grimy crust bit by bit. Her lips opened, gasping, and she licked up the melting liquid with the end of her tongue.

'I'll give you the bottle on one condition.'

'What's that?'

'That you completely stop from hatching that plot.'

'What do you mean?'

'Don't you realise that you are under surveillance and that your every move is watched carefully?'

'Surveillance!?'

'Every move, indeed every emotion.'

'Emotion?'

'Yes, you must forget everything about your mother, your aunt, Hathur, Sekhmet and all women. Yes, all women, do you understand?'

She nodded her head to indicate that she understood. But she did not understand anything. She wanted the bottle and nothing else. The man paced the ground, stirring up from it particles of oil. He brought the neck of the bottle near her lips. She consumed it with her teeth, shaking it a number of times. She bent over like an earthworm. Upside down above her mouth, the bottle was dry without a drop of water. Its base was thick and raised to heaven. The disc of the sun pierced through it directly into her eyes, as if it was an outstretched column of the everlasting fire.

She threw the bottle into the eye of the sun. The man shook his head in shame.

'Didn't you know that it was empty?'

'I knew, but ...'

'If we assume that a woman has a spirit like a man ...'

'Yes.'

'Then this spirit must live in her body.'

'Yes, but ...'

'But what?'

'After celebrating the Festival, little people like ourselves will be forgotten and the great will seize our portion.'

She was looking into his eyes and realised that he was covering something else with his words. He used to hide himself in the back room and take her portion. Then he would hide the bottle in a place that she did not know about. Would he try to dominate her through thirst?

The man was standing staring into space. He avoided looking into her eyes. Perhaps he knew everything. He was privy to the plot. At the decisive moment he would stand with His Majesty or at least with the boss of the company.

She froze at the door of the house twisting her neck towards the horizon. The clouds were piling up like black drops. There was nothing there to indicate that the storm had died down.

Her chest rose and fell in a deep sigh. With every breath, it seemed that her spirit was leaving her body.

She continued to keep her lips firmly closed in silence. Silence delivered her from nothing. She must expose the matter to the neighbouring women. Perhaps the women could do something. Yes, she could take refuge with the women.

She heard him cough with a sound like the creaking of the jar. She froze in her place with fear. Did the women know more than her? Could the women sacrifice her if that became necessary?

She remained standing where she was. She wrapped her arms around her chest like somebody feeling cold. Her eyes unconsciously darted to and fro. She moved forward a step and then back a step. Like a rat standing in front of a hole in the wall not knowing if it is a bolt hole or the mouth of a trap.

As she stood there, fatigue overcame her. Drops of sweat fell from her forehead. She licked them up with the tip of her tongue and savoured their moistness. She appeared to have regained some of her confidence.

She moved her feet and advanced towards the track. The disc of the sun was hidden behind the horizon. Winds were gusting from the north, raising particles of oil. On the edge of the lake she saw her sitting, undoing the black band above her face. She rubbed her nose and the corners of her eyes. Around her the women were doing the same, uncovering their faces. Each of them held her black band in her hands and then shook it in the air a number of times, making a sound like the crack of the wind. She began to advance on foot over the ground. She twirled round. Voices rose like the beating of a drum. Women were dancing in a circle, their feet advancing to the same beat. The singing rose to heaven with the dust.

***

'Is it our fate to carry on our heads ...'

'Jars of oil for ever?'

'No, sister! No, sister!'

'It's not our fate! It's not our fate!'

It was astonishing to see the wisps of light in the darkness. To discover the connection between fate and oil. Her body appeared to her like the wall, planted firm in the face of the storm. Nothing could topple her.

At that moment the man appeared raising his hand. The blow almost split her head open, but she jumped to escape death. He bent over her in a sort of fight. She threw him to the ground, even though she was worn out. He snatched the chisel from her hand, but she seized the jar by its two handles.

'Force is only defeated by force.'

The earth revolved around her as she fought. In a flash he came on top of her. He was so filled with illusory pride of possession that the hairs of his head bristled. Sticking up like that, they appeared like the crest of a rooster. The battle could have turned into something resembling love if she had not snatched the chisel from his hand.

She suddenly remembered that she bore the title 'researcher'. She had gone on leave. There was something she was searching for. The fever which had afflicted her body subsided. It appeared to her that the woman who had gone on leave was not the same one as the researcher. She could not love the man unless he submitted to her. If the movement of making him submit appeared to be innocent, it was not totally so.

With her other man, she had avoided this danger. She had been infected by an unknown virus that came under the heading of love. It was not a definite case of love, even though there was nothing to prove that it was not. At a moment when she was expecting to experience love, she had seen him grinding his teeth with intense hatred. Once he fell on her shoulder and took a great bite out of it. She had Iain in bed delirious. She had emitted sounds resembling the barking of a dog. The doctor had come and given her an injection in her thigh against rabies. He wrote something illegible on a piece of paper to the effect that she should abstain completely from love and from eating pickles soaked in oil.

'Can you see without pain?'

Yes, in the depths of her she was contented with him. She could look at him without pain. There was no alternative. Hope was totally lost and there was no alternative to writing the contract.

'Isn't the promise sufficient?'

'We must write a piece of paper.'

'Don't you trust me?'

'What do you mean?'

She signed the contract. The newspapers published much about cases of rape, rape of the body of course. Nobody had heard anything about something called rape of the spirit.

'Are you pissing standing up? That's forbidden for women!'

He had seen her through the crack in the door. It was not permitted for a woman to piss standing up. But she preferred to stand up. The toilet was flooded like a lake, and if she sat down, she was afraid that her body would touch the seat. The newspapers talked about the virus, which was passed on by sitting down, and by Satan as well. No sooner would the woman lift her dress than the virus would be standing in front of her in the form of a man.

'If a man and a woman meet together, the third among them is a devil.'

Sexual intercourse could not take place without Satan being present. Like walking in the darkness on the bridge. Satan would appear suddenly, standing with moustaches bristling like a hungry cat. Men and women equally were prisoners who had fallen into his clutches. They both suspected each other. Who had started it? Nobody knows exactly what had happened. And to establish innocence they write a paper. Anybody who does not know how to write hires a scribe. Scribes are many. Was there such a thing as a passion for writing?

'No, His Majesty himself doesn't know how to write.'

'What's the problem then?'

'Just regulations.'

'What do you mean?'

'If the spirit becomes inflamed, there are no boundaries that religion can set to its inflammation if there is no paper, and no regulations at all. Isn't that so?'

She did not reply. She had seen him through the crack in the door. She had been incapable of hiding. There is no room for movement when the net is rolled up. The net of heaven falls like black rain. In marriage also it appears that there is a net, and a stormy agitation of the spirit. There is nothing for the body to do but to submit. Or perhaps this is a strange idea. Perhaps the paper is the guarantee.

'There's no guarantee of anything.'

'What are you staying?'

'Everything has been turned on its head in an instant. I used to regard you as a young lady full of enthusiasm, and here you are an old woman. Can't you see yourself?'

The woman was lying in the empty space in front of the house. The edge of her cloak dangled over the edge of the lake. She looked at him wide-eyed, with the eyes of a frightened ox. The man stared at her with one protruding eye, the eye of a choked sheatfish. She rubbed the corners of her eyes with the edge of her finger. She looked at him carefully. Could a man like this be real? He seemed unreal to her, but nevertheless she continued to look at him. The oil continued to gush round her with the wind. It crept from under her cloak to the and advanced up her thighs. She began to resist the advance, but too late.

She jumped up, shaking off the black liquid. But it continued to advance despite her desires. It rolled up under the wall of the stomach and piled up on her arms and shoulders. She sobbed hoarsely. It became more determined. It advanced over her breasts and from there rose to her neck. Was it going to drown her?

'Unfortunately oil is not a man whom you can get rid of.'

She heard the strange voice piercing her body. It appeared as if it was her voice. Or the voice of her mother when she was inside the womb. It was apparently not her mother, but rather another woman who had borrowed her body. The period of loan had ended and the body had returned to its original owner. Perhaps she was deceiving herself simply to escape. But she had not forgotten the voice of her mother before she had been born. She was swimming in a gelatinous liquid. She was drowning in many dreams. The last dream was that she was pissing in the empty space, fearful that somebody would see her.

'I'm a respectable researcher.'

Yes, how often she had tried to tell him about herself. How

often she had tried to state to him the truth about herself, that she was a researcher in archaeology and that she had a husband waiting for her there. Her boss at work would confirm that she was competent, and her lady colleagues would certainly remember her. Could ladies lose their memory as well, as well as everything else?

'Isn't it just that you should pay me my wage? Is it possible for me to lose the sweat of my brow that I have shed all this time? And all I want is a return ticket.'

The man moistened his lower lip with his tongue, and smiled without looking at her. His smile simply appeared as wrinkles in the skin around the mouth. All she could do was hold on to the chisel. As she raised her arm, she let out a cry.

'Do you want to kill me?'

Her arm fell back and she did not speak.

'Definitely the conversation has come to an end.'

'We could begin again.'

'How's that?'

'We could reach for the lowest common denominator of agreement. We only have one goal, to protect ourselves from death. Isn't that right? Fortunately we are still strong. We have powerful arms and we can work. This is the goal of remaining here. In spite of everything, oil is better than other fiercer creatures. Oil can be friendly towards us if we surrender to it, but you never stop resisting it.'

Her eyes widened and she did not speak.

'All we ask for is mercy. We all know that the only person who benefits from the oil is the owner of the company, and His Majesty of course. That's logical. What's wrong with that? It's their right, by order of heaven. Do you never stop being greedy?'

She did not know definitely that it was the voice of the man. Perhaps the whole situation was returning to her imagination. Outside the voices of the women mumbled away, and their subdued staccato laughter sounded like sobbing.

'What's got into you, interfering in events that do not concern us?'

'What do you mean? Don't we carry jars?'

'Curse them. They have given us headaches and they will do away with us all.'

'There must be solidarity so that we can become powerful.'

'There is no power and no strength save in God.'

The man had begun to work. She saw him move his arms with new determination, and his muscles were bulging. He wiped away his sweat with the sleeve of his shirt, then stopped suddenly. He moved his head towards her. He saw her from afar talking to the women. The mouse was playing in the light of the sun and the hawk was hovering low on the horizon. It folded its big wings and concealed the sun. The woman looked at the clouds. Her face appeared pale, covered by black particles like freckles. Her eyes clouded over and the blood in her veins became red. Her bag opened suddenly with the force of the wind. She saw a long nose like that of a mouse playing with the contents. He took out the chisel, and began to search inside the lining. The wind rose and almost snatched her from her place. The waterfall gushed out all over her face. She wiped it away with the sleeve of and opened her eyes. It was not a mouse but the man. He was curled up on the ground like a caterpillar, searching through the pockets of her bag.

'You have no right to do that!'

'What's this paper?'

'I have my private papers.'

'Do you have another husband?'

He had strange-looking fingers. The paper was folded in the bottom under the lining. No finger could reach it without long training in the police academy. She reached out her arm and snatched the paper away. She thrust it down her throat and swallowed it. He attacked her with a sudden movement. He came on top of her and put his finger down her throat to pull out the paper. He felt around under the uvula and among the folds of flesh. His breath came out of his open mouth like steam coming out of the funnel of a steam engine. Then he finally pulled out his finger holding something small, resembling a bean or a congealed piece of oil.

'In spite of everything you deserve my thanks.' She said this in a voice laden with sincerity. Her body appeared more powerful. She inhaled and exhaled more easily. He had been able to rid her of that lump in the throat.

He appeared not to hear her. He was watching the movement of the paper inside her. Never before had he intended to deceive her in this way. He would watch her comings and goings from the toilet. That bit of paper would not escape him.

'Let's assume that it is a marriage contract. Then who's the man? And if it is not a marriage contract, what is it? A love letter?'

In his eyes love appeared less dangerous than marriage, for love was not binding. He took a cigarette out of his pocket. He flicked his fingers as he lit the match. He was sitting on a full jar. Circles of smoke spread around him. Then he raised his eyes to the horizon. The hawk had landed at the edge of the lake, and had begun to eat something small that twisted between its teeth like a caterpillar.

'If, when it comes down to it, it is simply a matter of love, then what sort of love is it?' This was the question he asked himself as he puffed out the smoke. He only knew one type of love. That for which you pay nothing.

The woman became tired of standing so she sat down on the chair. Behind the door he was watching her through the keyhole. Perhaps the paper had been totally digested or perhaps the words had disappeared as the ink ran. He saw her pressing on her stomach with her hands as if she was imprinting the words on the paper, protecting them from disappearing. Could one love to this degree!?

He heard her humming in a loud voice. She began to sing a song that she had sung in her childhood. She raised her voice and drowned the other voices in silence. Her song flowed out through the door. She had rescued the paper and the letters that were on it. The thought had come to her as she was sitting down. The night of the Feast would be the best night to flee. The man was going to the celebration. The invitation was from His Majesty and he could not absent himself. They would wear brilliant cloaks and new shoes and sit hour after hour behind locked doors. He could not go out even if he had indigestion. He would curl up in his chair hour after hour, and he might even piss a little before His Majesty arrived. One of them would feel the seat under him, and then stealthily put his finger to his nose. His eyes would widen in fright. It was not the smell of urine. On his finger he would see a layer of black, neither liquid nor solid. It had the smell of oil. But nobody could say anything. Each of them would wipe his finger surreptitiously on his *sarwal* and remain in his seat waiting for the doors to open.

'Perhaps she could cross the boundary before he returned from the celebration.'

The man remained transfixed behind the keyhole. He did not know exactly when he could swoop. The woman appeared to be sleeping as she sat. Her head dangled above her chest, and her eyes were closed. He was wondering which was more dangerous. If it was a love letter or a marriage contract. Perhaps he could uncover the two dangers at the same time, if the two men were in fact one and the same.

At that moment the storm rose and the keyhole became blocked. The way ahead of him appeared completely blocked and he could see nothing apart from darkness. He heard the woman as if she was laughing behind the door. Could there be a relationship between love and oil? The thought filled him with terror, and he stepped backwards, and found himself flat on his back.

The woman did not see him when he fell. She imagined he was still behind the door. Pain was tearing her insides apart. She was gulping down air. It was not a laugh or a broken sob. She wanted to cry out for help but remembered that he was behind the door and could attack her if he heard her voice.

'How can you pull the chain without making a noise?'

But of course there was no water there, and nothing to remove the traces. She did not want to open the door and go out brazenly. What disturbed her most was the smell. A mixture of sweat, oil, and remains of sardines and pickles. Was it a repulsive smell? Of course not. It was so familiar that she had feelings of love towards it. However, the man placed his hand over his nose and cried as if for help. She seized the opportunity and leapt out of the door.

The sun was just going down below the horizon. In the twilight she began to orientate herself on the ground. She found the patch of ground specified on the map. She raised her arm and hit the ground with the chisel time after time. Suddenly she felt it hitting against something solid. It was a small bronze statue. The breast was clear and did not brook any doubt. The bottom also confirmed that it was a woman. On her head she carried the disc of the sun and the horns tilted forwards. There was no doubt that it was the goddess Hathur. Who else could it be? There was a hole in her head and the skin was eaten away because of the oil and the underground sewage. However, the face was round; there was a smile on the lips and the chin and the nose were very delicate. There was a belt around the dainty waist and a snake wrapped and tied around the forehead. On her chest there was only one breast; perhaps the oil had eaten away the other one. However, the letters were carved on the rock and the name was set in a frame: the one-breasted god. Her eyes widened and she looked more carefully. She realised that one of the breasts had been removed by somebody. He had intended to remove the other but there had not been enough time. He had also tried to wipe off the smile, or to draw lines around the mouth to complete a frown, but the body remained as it had been, with a plump bottom and the spirit hovering around the one breast as if it was the breast of a mother.

'This statue will attract many tourists, wave after wave of them, and hard currency will pour in.'

'What are you saying?'

'Don't you understand my words? What's happened to you? Are you ill?'

'No, but I asked for leave.'

'What are you saying?'

'A simple request.'

'Are you out of your mind!?'

Her boss at work had not grasped what she was saying. She

had discovered signs of forgery, of goddesses being changed into gods. She could not talk to her husband about her boss at work. Her husband couldn't bear such conversation. Her boss could not bear to hear the name of her husband, and she could not bear to hear about either of the men. All that she wanted was a paper to write the request on, for there was no leave without a written paper specifying the date of departure, the date of return, and the destination. You could not leave the date of return unspecified. A man could absent himself for seven years and then return to find his wife waiting for him, by order of the law. However, the only leave the woman received was on the day of her funeral. How precarious was the distinction between leave and death.

The light over the oil dunes disappeared. The outline of the track was lost in the darkness. She stopped walking. The wind was whistling but she could not hear anything. The ear canal was completely blocked and she lacked her sense of hearing. Could she run away without making any noise? She looked at the watch on her wrist. The hour hand pointed to seven, the minute hand had stopped, and the second hand was totally decrepit. If only she could cross the boundary before sunrise. She would not try to hold on to oil like she had held on to love. The track ahead of her appeared slippery. The slope was steep and the dunes high. There was no difference between going up and going down. She abandoned her body to the movement as she had abandoned herself to it as a child. Her head beat against the darkness and her legs sank in above the knees.

Night came. The oil extended without end. Wave upon wave. There was no trace of the lights of the village. There were no houses and no bridge. She closed her eyes. She imagined her husband waking up from sleep and not finding her. He would crane his neck towards the door of the toilet. If it was closed, he would believe that she was in there, and if it was open he would think that she was in the bathroom, or perhaps in the kitchen. He could determine where she was without opening his eyes. If he opened his eyes, he could not see her except by going the other side of the door.

It had not occurred to him even in a dream that he could lose her. It was not permitted for a woman to be lost. She had no other place to lose herself in, and if there was another place, there was not another man, and if there was another man, there was no piece of paper. And a woman had no existence without a piece of paper.

'And he never doubted her existence, did he?'

When her husband stretched out his arm, he could catch hold of her, even when he was asleep. And when he was awake he could stretch out his leg and kick her. The place was so cramped, and it became even more cramped as time passed, the size of the body increased, the amount of fat increased and the amount of movement decreased. On the night of the Festival, he would carry her on his back, as if she was a lamb, and place her on the scales, and with the price he received he would buy that new machine.

'What is that machine?'

'That one that she taps on with her fingers and it writes without learning how to write.'

Yes, the dream was quite legitimate. The machine did not have a mouth like a woman to eat, nor a tongue to talk with. Moreover, it wrote in a clear hand. And if it was not writing, it stayed in its place without moving. If it became decrepit with time, it could be exchanged, and it would be possible for him to do without the woman entirely.

'It's a new type of machine, with buttons for writing and buttons for reading, buttons for brushing and buttons for wiping ...'

'And who will cook for you?'

'There's a white button which you press on and ask for any food you want. It'll give you a piping hot meal, along with salads, pickles and everything else.'

'And sex, I mean love?'

'It has another button for that, coloured red.'

The woman strained her ears, and voices came to her across time-consuming distances. She had been astute enough to be able to go on leave. Yes indeed, for the tame ox could go on leave for a day, and the machine could stop working for a day, and nobody could accuse either of them of immorality. But unfortunately she was a woman, and she could not be innocent. 'If a woman leaves her husband's bed for one night, she shall be hung by her hair on the Day of Resurrection and burnt in the fire.'

It was the voice of her husband in their days of love. He could not bear for her to be absent for a single night. But that was before those machines were discovered. And before oil became a power like electricity. She had been a placid girl, totally obedient to the orders of her husband and her boss at work. A respected and first-rate researcher. Her name was in the register with the picture of a mummy. Everybody had been pleased with her and she had had no enemies. Nor did she have any friends, because there is nothing that dirties the reputation of a woman as much as friends. Above all that, the only thing she was interested in was the exploration of archaeological sites.

'Gods? His Majesty? Didn't she have any interest in them?'

'What do you mean?'

'I mean, didn't she have any interest in politics?'

'Did you say 'politics'? Don't you know that it is forbidden for women to engage in politics?'

'Didn't she used to read the newspapers at least?'

'She couldn't read or write?'

'She was beautiful then.'

The conversation appeared strange to her, even though it was completely natural. However, the matter was not easy. A woman could not be beautiful apart from a very good make of mirror. And mirrors used to deteriorate with time. Black particles crept into them, borne on the gusts of wind. Her face would appear full of blemishes, and these blemishes would increase with the passing of time. They would spread over the nose and the cheeks, and climb to cover the forehead. They would blot out all her features, even the eyes. Nothing would be left apart from one or perhaps half an eye.

She froze, standing in her place. She saw her picture reflected on the ceiling. Was it her face? She could only see half an eye, and on her head a jar. Her neck was bent sideways. Could it be one of the neighbours and not her? She hit the mirror with her hand and broke it. Yes, what was the point of a mirror for a woman who no longer looked at her face?

'There must be a reason that forces a woman to conceal her face from the world.'

'Yes, of course.'

'This is an indication of the immorality of women.'

'Yes.'

'Good, then do you have any new information?'

'Not at all. They haven't found any trace of her yet.'

'What's this machine? It appears that you've bought a new typewriter.'

'Yes, it writes, sweeps, wipes, washes and cooks, and everything else.'

'Then you can travel and enjoy your leave. I have a rest house far away in the open country.'

'Do you mean Jar Sunira?'

'It now has a new name. Didn't you know that?'

'Yes, the Rest House, that's a better name, and I can pay you some rent, a nominal one at least.'

'I have no objection, if you insist. Prices have risen, as the price of a jar has risen.'

'Of course. This is also due to the immorality of women. Haven't you heard about that latest heresy?'

'Yes, women have begun to ask for wages.'

'That'll lead to an insane rise in prices.'

'Don't worry. There are new machines to take over the woman's role. They carry jars on four rubber feet, and walk by oil power.'

'This is God's favour upon us. Don't you see that God is always with us?'

★ ★ ★

She continued eavesdropping on the interrogation over the long distance. She stopped to wipe the sweat with her sleeve. Would it be better for her to return? She turned around, taking one step forward and then a step back. She stopped on the edge of the lake.

Her eyes looked towards the sky, watching as the lights appeared. Perhaps her childhood was the cause. She was unable to forget her childhood. At sunset she used to climb up onto the bridge and wait. Fields of crops stretched beside the river. At the bottom of the slope lay houses that were stuck together and leaning against each other. On the roofs were discs of dung, firewood, dovecotes and dusty ground, from which rose dust and the smells of mallow and dung. Flies and mosquitoes flew around them, and flying black cockroaches. Children were playing in the big lake behind the mosque. From it there rose the croaking of frogs and the sounds of crying and laughter. From the country track rose the voices of those returning from the fields. Their feet stirred up the dust, as did the pads of the buffalo and the oxen. The breath of the animals mixed with the breath of the human population. She was sitting on the bridge waiting. She followed with her eyes the quivering of the stars above her head. At the bottom of the slope, wisps of light quivered in the houses. The sound of neighing rang out freely in the darkness of the night, and the sad singing of women as they sat in the gloom with their backs against the wall. Her aunt had tied her head with a scarf, and was sitting on the bridge not wanting to return. She was wearing a *jallaba* whose bottom edge was spattered with mud. She wore it every day as she walked from the house to the field carrying on her head the sacks of vegetables. In the evening she would not play with the children, for playing was only for boys. For her there was nothing to equal sitting on the bridge with her eyes fixed on the horizon, her heart pulsing vigorously and the lights shining in the sky overhead. Lamps trembled in the windows, hung on poles surmounted by hooks, around which buzzed green moths with splayed feet. The clay benches were filling with men emerging from their houses and coming from the neighbouring villages, drinking tea and smoking, and passing on news from the newspapers. She closed her eyes and saw herself entering school and learning to read and write, and becoming a researcher in some branch of knowledge, or a secretary of the type whose pictures you see in the newspapers. The arteries in her neck were pulsing vigorously, as if thoughts of genius were pulsing into her head. Her aunt and all the women neighbours were raising their chapped palms upwards, beseeching the Lady of Purity to protect her from envy and evil spirits. She could hear their voices whispering with a sound like the rustling of wind, 'This girl has a world-class mind.'

In her childhood her head had become filled with this thought, and also innumerable other thoughts that poured into her from all around as she watched the stars. Under these lights, she saw life with the utmost clarity, like an open book, in total simplicity. She saw that death is simpler than life and begins at the moment of birth, that pregnancy accelerates death, that marriage is illogical, that kings and gods are villains and have committed many sins, and that she had witnessed the death of her father while she was a fetus in her mother's womb, and had been so happy at that event that she had slipped out of the womb.

At that moment she felt her body slip of its own accord under the bridge. When she returned to the house she would receive a heated telling off or would remain without supper. However, every sunset she would walk to the bridge, sit in her place there and wait for the stars to appear, as if she was discovering something new every time the lights appeared.

'What in the name of the Lady of Purity can any of us women lose?'

Nevertheless, none of the women thought of running away. She did not understand the mystery. Why was the woman forced to return when she would not lose anything if she did not return? Perhaps apart from a violent beating. But the women began to make off in the darkness. All she heard of them were distant whispers like the rustling of the wind.

'This woman is thinking of running away.'

'A woman without a mind.'

'Satan's got hold of her mind.'

'Rather it's the jar that heats up the mind.'

'Curses on that jar. It's a headache to all of us.'

'Have mercy on us, Lady of Purity.'

★ ★ ★

The man had returned suddenly. He began to lift the jar off the ground while she knelt down on her knees like a camel. With a single movement the jar came onto her head. All that separated it from her hair was the wase wrapped round and tied above the forehead. The heat began to seep through and her neck began to twist. She was wondering what she could lose. There was nothing that she could lose apart from that rubbing that occurred while she was asleep, when his arm reached out in the darkness and took hold of her hand, and she would abandon it to him simply because she was sound asleep. If she was not sound asleep, she would also abandon it to him, but with stabs of conscience. Then she would withdraw it from him with a yawn and turn over on the other side to face the wall.

'Is there not even the beginning of love between us?'

Perhaps that was his voice, or her voice. Both of them discovered this doubt too late. It had been clearly present right from the beginning. But everything was obscure and difficult to understand. Perhaps it was the oil or the heat in the head. Perhaps it was also the shyness that occurs when love is absent and when friendship between a man and woman is not there. If these are absent what can bring the man and woman together?

'What are you saying?'

'Pregnancy.'

The man was standing in his place with his shoulders drooping. His chest was bare against the night. She saw him tense the muscles of his face and open his mouth. A movement very similar to a smile of love. However, it was more ferocious than a wolf's snarl. He may get involved in acts of love, but that was only because of his despair, the intense heat or the swollen skin.

'Man is superior to woman, even in love.'

'Do you mean self-love?'

'Listen! What are those voices?'

She could not hear anything. Perhaps they were voices emerging from the past, or from an imagination affected by sunstroke. In spite of that she could understand the relationship between self-love and the sex instinct.

She raised her arm upwards and took hold of the bottom of the jar, afraid that it might fall. She plunged her feet in the well. As she plunged in she realised that there was something else in her childhood that she could not forget, namely the look in her aunt's eyes before the cart disappeared into the night with the dogs. The rain beat down more fiercely because of the wind, and the black particles were flying about more swiftly, resembling cockroaches flying in the night. In spite of the rain and the slipperiness of the ground, she had to carry two or three times the number of jars in the hope of obtaining a return ticket, or half a ticket. They may cut the price by half for child minors or for women of good reputation, or for sick or feeble-minded men.

She plunged in to the bottom fearlessly. She let the gushing waves of oil slap her chest and tear her *jallaba*. Her body became naked and twisted with the movement of the wave. She panted like a child swimming. Water entered her lungs and she groaned. She raised her arm and shook violently, in a dance like that of a chicken just after it has had its throat cut.

The storm died down a little, and her body became calmer as well. Her mind began to work. Yes, her mind had no other work apart from thinking about running away. She could have run away at that moment, except that her body was buried in the ground. The man also was standing above her head like a hawk. Her boss at work did not stop asking how many jars she had carried. Why are you late coming to work? There was a register to be signed on arrival and departure. She had to sign every day, on arrival and departure, and enter the number of jars that she had carried.

'Yes, if her body is buried in this place, why not begin digging immediately?'

She determined immediately to take up the chisel and begin searching again. She had no other goal apart from discovering her body. If she did not find the whole body, perhaps she would find a limb or two, or some remains. Perhaps chance would smile on her and she would discover a goddess as well. Enthusiasm poured into her like a surge of muscular energy. She pulled on the strap like someone who was about to hit two birds with one stone.

It was very hot. She took the bag off her shoulder, and the strap as well. She undid the buttons of her cloak and rid herself of her clothes completely. Her body appeared younger than she had imagined. The thought came to her that another body other than her own had slipped with its power into the space that she was occupying. In vain she tried to put her hand on it. There was someone holding her hand in his hand. Perhaps it was the man. Who else? He was telling her off because she had not prepared the supper. The evenings when he did not rebuke her, he used to go off into a deep sleep, without saying a word or even looking at her.

The heat did not disturb her, perhaps because she was naked. A slight breeze caressed her breasts. Her eyes widened as she saw that naked body. Her astonishment increased when she moved it the other way and it disappeared.

She had to move her head a little to see it again. A tall body with tort muscles, particularly her stomach muscles, no doubt because she had never been pregnant, and her neck muscles, no doubt because of the jars. Also the muscles of her right arm, no doubt because she had been digging with the chisel. Her fingers were long and tapering, suggestive of movement without actually moving, and her nails were black.

She had never previously considered her body from as close as this. The bridge of her nose was red and inflamed because of the sun and her eyelids were swollen. Her shoulders fell away sharply to right and left. They were a dark bronze colour like the colour of the mummy. Her real flesh began at the chest. Two breasts that stuck out proudly, hot as if heated from inside by a hidden spirit, and two coy nipples that beat with another pulse emanating from an unknown depth.

Her eyes followed on downwards and her body slipped away. They froze on a forest of hair below the stomach. She tried in vain to look. She had never been able to see clearly. If she tried to look closely, she felt her eyes becoming inflamed. She could never penetrate this forest, which appeared hollow to her, in spite of its thickness. Was that because of the emptiness of the world!?

What most used to disturb her was that she was incapable of gazing for a long time into her eyes. She saw them as hollow under the bone of her forehead that was as dry as the ground. She looked at them as if they were two remote spots on the horizon, more distant than the stars, as if they were the eyes of another woman looking out on her from behind the clouds.

'No doubt the eyes of a goddess.'

She had determined the place according to the map. She continued to dig throughout the day from sunrise to sunset. She had no doubt about the place. The smell of her body rose from the depths of the earth. There was nothing that indicated the body apart from the smell. However, by the end of the day, she had not come across anything. She came out empty-handed with the chisel.

Perhaps she had been mistaken about the place. There was nothing like a mistake for restoring hope to her. She picked up her bag and moved to another place which she imagined to be the right one. The smell rose more strongly from it. The stronger the smell became, the more convinced she was that she was near her body. She dug until she reached the bottom. She did not find anything and moved to another place. She was not prepared to accept despair. The day passed while she dug in vain. She continued day after day to hug hope to her bosom, and every day she moved from one place to another. Finally, when the last day came to an end and the sun set, her body collapsed in exhaustion and she burst into tears.

'Would it be better to go back to carrying jars?'

But tears flowed down like compressed steam. Her head was lightened somewhat from the pressure, and then she opened her eyes. She realised that her eyelids were swollen and that her tears had mixed with the particles of oil. However, her mind was strangely clear, and a thought came to her from afar like a star shining in the darkness of the night. The absence of goddesses in this place did not mean their absolute absence. Moreover, the earth rotates, so perhaps places are exchanged as the earth rotates.

'A totally logical thought.'

There was evidence in support of this thought. The position of her body had indeed changed. It was no longer in the place it had been in at the beginning. The gushing waterfall had swept her to another place. And in the depths of the earth, the current was also keeping people's remains in continuous motion. In this way it would be possible for her remains to cross the border, if it were not for the checkpoint, unless of course the guard was sound asleep.

Perhaps it was her bad luck. The guard was awake, for no other reason than that the mosquitoes were awake. The pesticides also were cheated for the mosquitoes gobbled them up in the twinkling of an eye, and one of them would become the size of a frog. Yes, some of the bodies could manage to get through passport control. Perhaps her body would have been successful in running away without a ticket or written permission in her husband's handwriting, or a yellow paper stamped with the hawk and the signature of her boss at work. She had no intention of breaking the law. She was a model of obedience and fidelity. It would at least have been possible for her remains to pass without tests, if it was not for the establishment of the building that was later called the pathology laboratory. In her dreams at night, she could not look at her body stretched out on the cold marble operating table, her nose full of formalin.

She felt a cupped hand rocking her. It was of course the hand of the man. Who else could it be? His voice in her ear was as gentle as the breeze, 'When it comes down to it, the smell of formalin is no worse than oil.'

He was totally truthful in what he said. The smell of formalin seemed more delicate. Or perhaps it was the dream, since in dreams things become more beautiful simply because they do not really exist. A thought came to her that she must be beautiful now in the eyes of her husband simply because she was not there.

Following a violent blow she was thrown to the ground and lost consciousness. She could not keep her feet fixed in their place. The current dragged her off in a direction she could not determine. Before she could recover her senses a sound like the siren of a boat rang out. She was being rushed along towards the shore, and she began to hear the sound of waves, like drums.

'Help!'

The cry broke from her like the sound of a slaughtered animal. She could have lived like the other women, and then died, if it had not been for that chisel and those sunset sessions on the bridge when she was a child, and that light. Enough! Enough! There was no point now in anything.

'Help!'

Her voice rang out like a whistle amidst the beating of the drums, or the whistle of silence that rings in the ear before the last breath. Apart from the fact that she was seeing the sail from afar. A white dot on the horizon. It was the first time any boat had appeared on the sea. Her eyes discovered the light. A spot of great clarity. As clearly defined as a drop of water. Clear and pure and sweet like the voice of her mother entering her ears before she was born.

'Hold my hands!'

She saw a long arm with five fingers extended at full stretch towards her. She stretched out her arm as she used to do when she was a child. Her eyes were fixed firmly on the point of light. She jumped forwards shaking with intoxication. The voice in her ears was as clear and as definite as the stars.

'Put your hand in mine.'

She moved her body so as to stretch out her arm further. The voice disappeared as if the movement had dispelled it or as if it had been drowned out by the din of the drums and the barking of the dogs in the distance. Darkness fell resembling the cavity of the womb. She realised that her mother must have lived this moment, when the sun was setting and the universe was drowning in darkness. She used to sit like her on the bridge. Her eyes were alert and when the lights appeared, her body trembled as she used to tremble, and her heart beat vigorously, on the point of discovering the thing that always used to appear as if it was nothing.

The lake stretched endlessly before her eyes. The man had turned round and returned to the house. His back had become humped after having collapsed in bed. He was sleeping heavily and she was lying down with eyelids closed. In her dreams, she never stopped running away. She surrendered her legs to the wind. Behind her there was something running on two legs, or sometimes four or six. She was not able to count the legs or the paws. The sound of panting behind her was loud. It had a regular rhythm like snoring. When she turned round, she could not see anything running behind her apart from her black shadow on the ground.

'Are you awake?'

'No, asleep.'

She did not know how he could reply to her while he was asleep, but he used to talk in his sleep more than any other time. If he turned over on the other side, she did not hear any sound. It was hot, as if the disc of the sun had not set. The darkness was so intense that it was almost palpable. The light of the lamp was almost spent, although it remained steady. Nothing moved apart from those winged creatures. It was natural for white moths to be drawn to the light. But these creatures were not white. And they were not as small as moths. They were as big as frogs, as black as night.

'Does oil also change the nature of moths?'

The frogs began to orbit swiftly around the lamp. She gazed at one of them for a long time. It had a black head as if it were tied round with a scarf. Its mouth was fixed without a smile, beating time after time against the lamp. Its shadow on the wall behind was bigger than its real size, and danced as it moved, staggering like a chicken with its throat cut. It kept banging itself and was being drawn ceaselessly towards the flame, clinging to it and trying to steady itself on it for fear that it might fall.

It seemed to her to be an intelligent frog, in spite of its crazy longing. Did she not have anything to hold on to apart from what destroyed her? She was longing to be rescued, even though rescue was no other than death. The flame had afflicted her with a fever in the head, and it fell singed to the ground like a grilled fish. Her eyes protruded, filled with regret. She stretched out her arm to pat its head, and suddenly there rose from it the smell of grilled meat. With a swift movement of her hand she put it in her mouth and swallowed it in a moment. She did not have time for pangs of conscience.

The man looked at her as she licked her lips after the appetising meal. She wiped her mouth with her sleeve as if to conceal the sin. She tensed the muscles of her back. She began to move her feet as she used to do when she was a child. She quickened her pace. As if to meet a particular appointment at a particular place.

She began to pant like a child. She almost cried out with joy when she arrived a moment before the time of the appointment. That night there was a storm and the black dust covered the sky and the earth. She continued to sit in her place waiting. Perhaps she remained waiting for half the night. She was certain that the women were there behind the clouds and that they would appear as they did every night. When she saw the clouds moving, she would move from this place to another place. The women will appear. They definitely will appear. She began to sing to amuse herself. She heard her aunt and the neighbour women singing to the Lady of Purity, or singing to the rising sun, or the wheat at harvest, or the waters of the Nile when they are in Rood, or the moon when it becomes full. Her eyes lost themselves in the vastness of the pitch-black darkness. Tears glistened in her eyes. The women had not appeared as they did every night.

'Had they betrayed her to His Majesty?'

The wind slapped her face with black particles. Everything around her was covered in darkness. It was not liquid and it was not solid. It crept in under the skin and entered the pores of her body. It penetrated under the bones to the sensory and nerve centres.

'Moisten your tongue with a drop or two.'

The man was standing up with his arm stretched out towards her with the bottle. She was trying to stretch out her arm. Her eyes were wide open, her lips were moving without letting out a sound, her ears were blocked, the particles piled up and melted with the heat, like black wax. He was standing in front of her at arm's length. His hand held the bottle. Her arm was stuck to her body. She tried to move it, but it would not move. Her body was firm in its place, while the frogs flew lightly around the lamp.

Her eyes widened, staring at the light. Her eyelids were inflamed and she could not close them. The flame burned the naked white. She closed her eyelids and pressed her eyes shut. Darkness seemed to be better than light. Her mind also seemed to her to be bigger than the mind of the frog. From under her eyelids she could see spots of light swimming in black spaces like drops of water slipping out from under her eyelids.

'Are you crying like other women?'

She did not know that it was her who was crying. Her sobbing was echoing in her ears and made her sound as if she was one of the neighbours. Or like her aunt, or her mother when she herself was still in the womb. Or perhaps the Lady of Purity herself. She had never heard the voice of the Lady of Purity. But her aunt used to hear it, and when she used to go to sleep, she used to leave the window open, and strain her ears just before dawn, and the voice would come like a ray of light that she could scarcely hear as she lay there. She would jump up and crane her neck towards the horizon, and the voice would come to her from afar before the light of dawn appeared.

'I have given the command for you to be healed from your headache. Get up!'

Her aunt would get up immediately from where she was lying. She would undo the scarf from around her head and sit in the tub. She would pour water over her body with the jug. As she poured each jug, she would invoke the Lady of Purity three times in a whisper.

'Who is the Lady of Purity, Auntie?'

Her aunt would open her arms as if she was the whole world. The Lady of Purity is the mother of the universe. She is the mother of heaven and earth. She is the only one capable of healing her. She is the mother of all gods and prophets. She is the giver of life and health. She is the goddess of sickness and death. 'Yes, my daughter, the one who gives life is also capable of taking it away. And the one who brings illness is also the one who brings healing.'

* * *

From behind the high sand dunes, across the great distance of the night, she saw the police commissioner sitting. He was in the same swivel chair, spinning it so that he was facing her husband. He looked as if they had woken him suddenly from sleep.

'I see that your eyelids are swollen and your lips are cracked. Are you ill?'

'Since the Festival they have not sent us the grant.'

'Will you never stop complaining, even in your old age? Don't you know that His Majesty is the faithful servant who is always vigilant in guarding our tranquillity?'

'Yes, that is totally clear, but ...'

'You've no excuse now for not writing, now that you have that new machine.'

'Is the company intending to bring us electricity?'

'Yes, when it comes, you can write even when there is a power cut. As you know, this new machine thinks, writes, sweeps, wipes and ...'

'And washes and cooks and everything. It performs the work of four wives at least.'

'Hasn't your wife returned from her leave yet?'

'Do you mean the first or the last?'

'In any case, we're serious in our search for her. We have to submit a report to His Majesty before the end of the Festival. As you know, he's waiting for your new article in honour of his birthday party. Do you know that he asked me about you? Why don't you write anymore?'

Since he had stopped writing, there had been nothing but worldly emptiness. Night extended into day and nobody asked after him. Spaces of darkness filled only by sleep. Or reading the newspaper, or moving his arms and legs in the air, and cracking his toes. Like His Majesty, he knew neither how to read nor write. It was not for him to try and outdo the King. Moreover, what was the point of reading and writing? All the prophets were illiterate, but in spite of that they could lead the world, couldn't they?

He was tapping with his fingers all night. The tapping beat inside her head as she slept. The wind was howling as well, and the waterfall roared like rain beating on the windows and the doors. She wrapped her head in the black scarf, and tied it above her forehead like a snake's head. She saw herself in the mirror, like the goddess Sekhmet. She stared at herself with red eyes, swollen at the corners.

'Are you awake?'

'No.'

She mouthed the word. She dosed her eyes, pretending to sleep. She studiously shut her eyelids, but he stretched out his arm. He tried to open her eyes with his fingers. As if he would put drops in them. Nothing poured into her eyes apart from the light of the lamp. It fondled the white of her eye like a flame. He was sitting in his place covering his upper half with the newspaper.

'Naturally, you feel embarrassed when you read your article, don't you?'

'Don't speak to me in that disrespectful way. Don't you know that I'm your husband?'

'No, I didn't know.'

'Don't you know that God has ordered the woman to prostrate herself before her husband? Come on, prostrate yourself before me, woman!'

'Don't you know that you prostrate yourself before His Majesty?'

'What's shameful in that? Everybody prostrates themselves before him.'

'Didn't he announce that you had received a bribe from the devil to stop writing about him?'

'That was nothing more than a gentle rebuke from His Majesty, and I wrote a complaint to him.'

'You complained to him about him?'

'What's shameful about that? Everybody complains to him about him. Come on. Take off your dirty cloak, take a shower and let's celebrate the Festival. Instead of one bottle we have two bottles. Look!'

★ ★ ★

He was holding a bottle in each hand and spinning round, beating the ground with his feet to a dance tune. The festival drums were beating out the same tune. The earth shook under his body, and his waistband came undone. His *sarwal* slipped to his feet. He kicked it with his right foot and it flew in the air and then caught a hook on the ceiling. It remained hanging there swinging under the light, covered with black stains and exuding a smell of oil. He continued to dance, naked as the day his mother gave birth to him. He did a complete turn and returned to exactly the same place where he had begun.

She had thought that he was still a youth, but his naked body revealed that he was an adult. His shoulders drooped downwards. His chest was bowed under a thin coat of hair. His muscles were like slack rope and his skin was as dry as a layer of plaster of Paris that one could peal off.

Her eyes followed the outline of his body downwards as it tapered off below his stomach. An oblique light fell on a mass of hair that shook at every breath, casting its shadow on the wall. The artery of his neck was swollen and pulsating. The pale light drew it with a black line. Yes, there was real oil in his neck. In that swollen artery and in that black liquid, which flowed like blood.

She remained standing, gazing around, fully dressed. He was looking at her expecting her to take her clothes off. However, she had begun to have doubts about him. She did not know that she had to strip like him. Her only aim in staying with him was to be protected behind a wall. If the waterfall caused the wall to fall down, then there would be nothing between them.

'OK. If the wall collapses, everything else will collapse as well.'

Perhaps she took a long time to strip. Everything happened as if it was nothing. Then the whistle rang in her ears like a scream. A scream of pain, totally black and utterly despairing. A scream without bounds, which cut through the darkness like the edge of a sword. It carried with it all the pains gathered from the expanse of the lake, and the depths of earth and heaven. Like the back of an animal laden with all the pains of the world, with the memory of humiliations and blows, celebratory parties, bottles, articles, flashing lights, mud, and all the suppressed longings for death and for return to the mother's womb.

Everything began to come to light in the light of the scream. The moon which was rising in the heavens. The wind which was ruffling the surface of the lake. Nakedness reaching the nadir of despair. Sweat feverish with hope. Memories of an obscure childhood. An unknown room in a previous life. The chisel of a researcher without any research to do. Goddesses without any existence anywhere. Small limbs scattered around, which can only be gathered by a supernatural power, gathering them and making them into those rays that stretch from her eyes to the surface of the moon.

'Is it the end of the world?'

'Rather it is the spirit of the Lady of Purity hovering around.'

She said it without opening her lips. Since her abortive flight she had almost forgotten everything else. Her whole life was pointless. However, her perspective on the affair changed as she moved her eyes. She saw the spirit hovering over the surface of the moon. She realised immediately that the moment had come. And she had chosen to carry out her mission. She tensed her muscles and sprang up. She quickened her pace along the path. Over her shoulders was her bag hanging from the strap. She grasped it with her hand as if she was pulling her existence out of nothing.

'OK. She has made her choice and now she has to lead the women to the way of salvation.'

'What are you saying, sister?'

'There is undoubtedly a path.'

'Haven't you become pregnant yet?'

'It isn't easy to find a man capable of love.'

In the depths of her she longed for love. The other women had husbands and children. Each one of them could list the names of her children on her fingers. Their eyes were full of indifference to everything. They no longer had hope in life, for what had it achieved for them? She had not found anything, but at least she was not ashamed of uncovering her face, and looking unreservedly into the light of the moon.

'Was it because of this that she had never in her life seen the man of her dreams?'

The man was standing in the doorway. She did not open her mouth. Even if she had said anything he would not have been able to understand, and if by any chance he had understood, fate would inevitably intervene to separate them. They were living within a system governed by fate. And fate only recognised one type of love. That fierce passion for the land and His Majesty. Perhaps that was because of the boundaries imposed by the oil. The strength of ebb and flow hidden in black waters, the roar of the wind and the movement of the waves and the gushing of the waterfall. It was certain that the man standing in front of her was not the man of her dreams. Both of them came from opposing points of the compass to meet by chance. As if all that had brought them together was fate.

★ ★ ★

'Nor was she an excellent cook. She was a woman without value who tried to derive her value from the value of goddesses.' It was the voice of her husband, or perhaps her boss at work, describing her to the policeman. On her way to work, she sometimes used to pass in front of a kitchen, and notice onions hanging in the window. The sight would strike her like the stab of a dagger. She would long to die before one hair of those head-like bulbs was touched. In her dream the yellow hairs of the onion heads appeared to her like snapping teeth, grabbing her neck from behind and throwing her the other side of death.

'Perhaps she needed some leave to take a holiday.'

The woman did not have the right to take a holiday. It was as if when the door opened and she went out, she would not return. The thought of love came to her. A great love deserving the death of a woman who had not known love, a woman who had dwelt in a perpetual prison. The non-existent wind, the smoke and the black particles, the silence and the rustling of the pages of the newspaper. The lower half of a sleeping man, and the kitchen. Yes. An aroma of grilled meat might waft from the kitchen and the man would wake up. Appetite would awaken and perhaps love would as well. However, the place itself never used to change. She was pushed into him by virtue of her instinct of self-preservation. The meals were never-ending, but they were not sufficient to quench desire. Yes, there was paper and the typewriter. She tapped out the request with her fingers.

'Did she request a holiday?'

'Yes.'

'Had she obtained the agreement of her husband?'

'No.'

'How did she manage to go on holiday then?'

Silence reigned in the interrogation room. The policeman spun round in his swivel chair. He turned on the red light. He kicked out the journalists. He typed a bit more, then spun round. He stared into the faces of her husband and her boss at work. 'Do you want me to be honest?'

'Yes.'

'Won't the news leak out to the newspapers?'

'Definitely not!'

'OK. Her need to go away was a desperate one.'

'What do you mean?'

'She went away to look for her lost pride. Hers was the pride of an animal who had set herself up on two legs and no longer crawled around on four legs. Indeed, she was not a woman of the kitchen or the bed. She did not memorise the tunes that the women sing in the public baths. And she was not aware of the love that arose in the heart of her husband when he saw her stuffing the cabbage. And more than that, her eyelashes did not flutter when her boss at work or His Majesty looked at her.'

The policeman's fingers froze on the typewriter. He erased the phrase 'His Majesty' and continued to type with one hand, while with the other hand he wiped the sweat from his face.

'A woman whose eyes are as hard as granite and cut from a mountain of cold ice.'

At this point the policeman stopped typing completely. He spun his body around a number of times in the chair and then came to a standstill. His face was facing the wall. He did not know exactly who was speaking. Her boss at work or her husband. He did not try to spin the chair round. He continued to stare at the wall, giving his back to the two men.

'What do you mean by this cold ice?'

'I mean that they were two eyes.'

'OK.'

Her husband exchanged glances with her boss at work. It seemed as if each one of them was trying to imagine the appearance of her eyes. Her boss at work puffed out a dense cloud of smoke from his pipe. Her husband shook his knees and then lowered his eyelids.

'I mean that they were nonchalant eyes. They did not look at you. And if they did look in your direction, it was with a look that went beyond you to a point on the distant horizon beyond your head.'

'Did she ever look at another man?'

The policeman spun round to face the two men with a look that cut like a sword. They looked at each other before replying together, 'No, she never used to look at other men. Perhaps for this reason they used to arouse both of us with a desire to slap them so that they would look at us. Yes, you could say that they were impudent eyes, eyes that were nonchalant towards you and me, while paying close attention to everything else, even if it was nothing, a mere dot infinitely small on the horizon.'

Silence reigned for a long time in the interrogation room. All that could be heard was the rising and falling sound of the three men's breathing, and the humming of the fan as it spun, and the sound of a fly as it buzzed round and bumped against the red light, and the sound of black particles like a drizzle of rain beating against the window.

The sounds filtered through to her over the great distance. They all dissolved into one sound with a regular rhythm. The policeman's silence rang out in a clear manner. She realised that he knew everything. His fingers began to type once again.

'What did her neck look like?'

'Er ... her neck. This too had a strange appearance, longer than any other neck, as if it was the skyline, rising like the neck of the griffin, a neck that you could not get a hold of in order to strangle it for instance. A neck that aroused your desire, in that you could not dominate it. A neck that was about to ...'

Silence fell. The fingers stopped typing. The chair spun round then stopped. All that could be heard was the sound of panting.

'About to what?'

'About to change into its opposite with a sudden movement, twisting and bending in surrender as if carrying a heavy weight.'

'An awesome thing.'

'Yes indeed. There is no doubt that you would tremble before this neck.'

'And what about the rest of her body?'

'That also was awesome.'

'What do you mean?'

'You would see her body existing indubitably in front of you. An existence that was unendingly present, but that would suddenly vanish to become a quasi-eternal absence.'

There was total silence. Not even the three men's breathing could be heard. Perhaps the fan also stopped, or there was a sudden power cut. The lamp went out and the fly flew away or burnt up. All that was left was the drizzle striking her ears with the same rhythm as the pulse of the arteries of her neck, and the whistle of the wind from afar like the silence of the night.

Then a laugh came to her through the darkness. She did not know which of the men was laughing. A strange staccato laugh like sobbing, high-pitched, resembling the sound of a man guffawing. His body shook because of the head shaking with laughter.

The guffaw came to her from beyond the dunes and the expanse of the lake, resembling the roaring of the wind. It beat against the walls like a drizzle of hail. It filtered under the door with the trickle of black oil. Her face was turned to the wall and her head wrapped in a scarf. With a ninety degree movement of her neck, her head came to face the door. The man was standing with his *jallaba* tucked up. His head was wet as if it had been soaked by the rain. He shook his hair and his whole self like a frog coming out of the lake. Her eyes met his and there he was, revealing the whites of his eyes with the movement of the wind, hiding the surface to reveal the hidden depths.

'Are you awake?'

His tone was delicate and controlled, bearing the tenderness of the man when he loses control of his woman. He took off his clothes with the movement of someone trying to strip off a humiliation. He was tall, and his skin was wet and stretched as if made from real leather, glistening in the darkness like a shoe wiped in the rain. He moved towards her with the step of someone who wants to assert that he owns something that he does not possess.

* * *

'Men are machines for concealing reality, who imagine in their hearts that they possess reality.'

'Are they gods?'

It was the voice of a woman talking to the other women. It resembled her voice when she was young. Each of them nodded in comprehension.

'We all understand that, sister, but the onion heads are still in the kitchen. No hand has touched them, it is almost time to eat, and the man is shouting. This is clear. Do you understand, sister?'

'Yes, I understand, sister, but frogs have evolved and have emerged from the bottom of the lake into the tight, while you women are incapable of movement.'

Silence fell when the man returned. He shouted as usual demanding food. Then he lay down naked in bed. He stretched out his arm in the darkness under the cover, as if he was stretching his hand underwater. His fingers tried in vain to reach her hand. Finally they reached it across the great distance. She was facing the wall. She felt his hand grasping her, rough and moist with black sweat. The whirlpool bore her to the depths of the earth. His chest was solid, like the chest of a mummy, hollow inside, filled with the emptiness of the world. But there was no escape. She had to put her head on this rock-like chest. As if it was the chest of the god Ekhnaton after they had removed his breasts.

'What are you saying, sister?'

'I've realised too late that everything is real. I mean marriage, and perhaps also the search for goddesses, and everything else in life, including death.'

'And love?!'

'No, I don't love him. If I loved him, the world would be submerged in fantasy.'

Her body was naked, in contact with the naked world, in all its reality, like flesh. She could have slipped from the bed and fled, but getting out of that well was impossible, or perhaps the oil appeared to her to be better than anything else.

She bent her arm in the narrow space. She choked with the smoke and the black dust. Death appeared to her to be a type of eternity, and flight appeared to her to be no more than stupidity. Indeed, death was the genius of the living being when it becomes eternal like the gods.

She pretended to be dead as she lay there. Her body fell into the depths without her bending her other arm. The darkness resembled an immense black eye. An eye that never stopped looking at her. A holy eye that never slept. It must be the eye of the goddess of death Sekhmet, or perhaps the eye of the Lady of Purity looking at her and reminding her of the entrusted message.

★ ★ ★

She opened her eyes suddenly. The man was staring at her from behind the newspaper. His eyes passed through the paper and penetrated her.

'Yes, she was under constant surveillance.'

'By order of His Majesty?'

'Perhaps, or perhaps it was her boss at work, or her husband. He hired a man to watch her in return for a sum of money. Or perhaps there were three of them - nobody knows exactly. But the surveillance was continual, twenty-four hours a day.'

The policeman was with them of course, spinning his chair and typing on the typewriter: 'She met with the women at six-thirty without obtaining permission to meet. She returned home at one-fifty. She drove the vehicle herself without depending on a male driver. All that constitutes a danger to the world order, demanding life imprisonment with hard labour, and the carrying of weights on her head. The matter of course demands that she be dismissed from work and divorced from her husband. If she wasn't married, His Majesty could have delegated the public judge to sentence her to death.'

The bed shook in the darkness whenever the man turned from side to side. Groans arose from the wooden planks like the meowing of a cat. With his nose he smelt the aroma of the food. No smell of food was coming from the kitchen. The onion heads were still lying in the sink. The stove was turned off and the aluminium vessel was empty. Its bottom shone under the light with a steely sparkle.

'Aren't you cooking?'

From the back of her neck she felt herself being pulled violently beyond the verge of consciousness. Slaps rained down haphazardly on her cheeks, her nose, her lips, her breasts, and her stomach. She could not open her eyes to see what was happening. It was the first time in her life that a man had hit her.

'Aren't you going to cry out for help?'

Perhaps it was one of the neighbours coming to see what the noise was. But it was certainly not her who had cried out. Or rather she had cried but no sound had come out. She wanted to conceal the matter in silence. She left her body stretched out on the ground. One of her legs was enwrapped in the strap of the case. She was totally naked apart from the remains of her torn *sarwal*, which encircled her foot like an anklet. Embroidered round the borders were her name and the name of her husband enclosed in a heart-shaped frame.

In the pale light her thighs appeared to her vast as if she was looking at them through a magnifying glass. Long and stretching out so far from her that she could scarcely see them over the long distance, as if they were the thighs of another woman.

Her eyes rose over her body, widening as they rose. They stopped as if stupefied in front of her head, which was dangling above her neck, a black scarf tied around it. Her swarthy face became even swarthier in the dim light, covered as it was with black particles like freckles, and lines like wrinkles drawn with a pen falling away from the corners of her swollen eyelids like black tears, and eyelashes lowered as if they had been transferred from youth to adulthood with a sideways movement of her eyes. She jumped up, tensing the muscles of her arms and legs. She pulled the depths of her inner mind from the caverns of the earth. She remembered that she had seen this face before, and lived through this moment in a previous life. This spectacle of punishment was something she had seen in both waking and sleeping dreams.

'It is shameful for a respectable woman like her to search for goddesses.'

She heard her voice sobbing. I want at least to die from shame. Then she suddenly silenced her sobbing and a voice came to her resembling the voice of one of the women.

'OK. What's the problem then? He always beats me and is puffed up with pride. Morning will not come before I have opened the door and left. Yes, I know. I will leave tomorrow, so wipe away those black tears. The world will not be overturned because a woman lay with a strange man in a passing liaison.'

Her voice changed with every movement of her body, and her body transferred from cold to hot as she turned from side to side. Her smell spread from a depth inside her that she could not probe. The smell of flesh lying in the depths of the earth. Perhaps she wanted to die in that moment. Or she did in fact die — then the tip of her nose touched the tip of his nose, and he withdrew himself from on top of her. Only at that moment did she realise that her body existed and that she had not died yet.

'Was that love?'

Dampness pervaded her from under the cover with the trickle of oil. It was sufficient for her to see this trickle of oil to realise that she was without value, and the distant smell was sufficient to purify her from sin. Her mouth like a chimney was puffing out clouds of smoke and the earth was swaying underneath her like water. She was a piece of dryness plunging to the bottom, anchoring her feet to the bottom of the earth.

'A woman fallen to this degree.'

'What do you mean?'

'Don't you know what I mean?'

'Have you got me under surveillance?'

'Yes. If I hadn't, I wouldn't have seen you with the other man.'

'And I saw you. Have you forgotten?'

'Of course you did. That's natural. And instead of one wife, God will give me four. Don't you know that?'

He was standing up, stretching his neck, full of pride. As the number of women in a man's life increases, so his neck gets longer. His neck stretched out endlessly like the skyline. It was a scene that terrified her more than death. It put her and the man in a world that was swaying. A house standing on water. A set of scales whose pans sway back and forth without coming to rest.

He was standing looking upwards. He blinked repeatedly. He tried to grasp heaven with his eyes. As if it was the only thing capable of being grasped in the expanses of fantasy.

She was still lying in her place. With her hands, she caressed her cheeks, which were swollen from the slaps. She looked at him out of the corner of her eye as he stood there. He was near the door, no more than a few steps away from her. He appeared very far away, as if he was absent.

'How can a man who has been so close as this withdraw to such an infinite distance because of one simple sideways glance on her part?'

'It's totally natural. A woman like you who exceeds all bounds with her sin can overturn the established order with the blink of an eye.'

'Is the established order so dilapidated?'

He did not have the energy to reply, but his heart quaked inside him. As if it had been fearing this movement all his life. What could wipe away this sin except for the woman to kneel before him. To wet his feet with her tears and ask his forgiveness. As her ignominy increased, so did his pride. For there is nothing that reduces the pride of a man like a woman without sin to fill her with regret.

He was standing waiting for her to kneel or to burst into tears, to gasp out her repentance and her remorse. However, she remained as silent as the dead in their graves. Threatening her with the punishments of earth and heaven did not succeed. All he could do was wait. However long it took, he would wait, for the only thing that could rescue his pride was for her to let some words like' Forgive me!' escape from her lips.

'Were his eyes imploring?'

Of course. With one movement of her eyes the situation was transformed. It was as if with her eyelids she was turning the pages of a picture book. In this picture he appeared bent low, kneeling in front of her, wetting her feet with his tears, begging her to say the words 'Forgive me!'. She wanted to open her mouth and ask his forgiveness, but to no avail. Her lips were stuck with oil, like gum.

Her eyelids also were stuck, like her lips, and her eyelashes were stuck together too.

Before her eyes, all she could see was darkness. When would these black clouds move far away and the lights appear? If the lights had appeared there, why didn't they appear here? If the sin had occurred here, why was it subject to punishment there?

The door opened with the force of the sudden wind. The waterfall of oil gushed in with a roar. The black dunes towered up between earth and heaven. The man raised his arm as a sign of despair. He realised that he had lost his opportunity, that his emptiness had been revealed to the eyes of the whole world, and that there was no hope of concealing the truth.

'Was that due to the oil gushing in at an unsuitable time?'

He was talking to himself with his arm upraised. As if he was addressing the peaks of the dunes or an unspecified force in heaven.

'O Oil! If you don't submerge her totally until she's dead, nothing will be left in this world of the pride of man.'

Apparently, the oil responded to the man's plea. The oil poured down with greater power, and the woman flailed around with her legs and arms to resist drowning. Of course, the oil could not abandon its nature and take sides with the woman. The man was convinced of this.

'Won't you apologise for your sin, woman?'

'I tried but ...'

'Has this happened before?'

'Yes, it has happened before ...' She said this with her eyes getting wider between heaven and earth. Unwittingly, she exchanged glances with the man. In the faint light she saw glances being exchanged that destroyed any remaining hope. Had she had life before? However, the question was beyond the strength of her imagination. The man had realised that she had been a sinner all the time, from birth until death.

'Of course, I knew that. What's new about it?' He said that as he climbed a long ladder to the roof. His cast-off was still swinging on the hook. His arm was stretched out trying to reach it. From behind he looked hump-backed like a camel. He was bow-legged and his legs were covered in fine hair, which was soaked with black sweat and matted together.

'Now she has to take the decision. If she doesn't, she will never take it.'

This was how things seemed to her. To stay forever or to return straight away. It was the first critical decision she had had to make in her life. Was it the oil that had forced her to make it? Or perhaps the memories of her old life made things seem more rosy than they had been. Although the slaps were a memory like the black marks, nevertheless woman-beating was a natural thing. The man had not stopped calling upon heaven to help him. Heaven whispered to him from on high, 'Beat them! She cannot expect a better future unless she accepts a beating with pride. She made her head like the head of the goddess Sekhmet, which was made of bronze. She entered the kitchen holding her neck haughtily like the goddess Nefertiti. She stood in front of the fire inhaling smoke into her bowels as if they were the bowels of the earth. She stored pain as if she was pregnant with it, then perfumed herself on the outside to conceal the smell. She resisted the desire to raise her arm to slap the man, and smiled in his face like an angel.

'Have you got two faces, woman?'

'You have double that, don't you? Four faces.'

The oil was still gushing out powerfully. It was pushing her once again to do something she did not want to do. She was totally incapable of comprehending what sublime love was, and what base love was. Since childhood she had understood important things that nobody else had understood. In vain she had tried to search for what she wanted to search for. The man was no more than a hindrance in her life, like the dunes of oil.

'He is a model man who is only responding to heaven's behest that he beat women.' This is how she comforted herself. In the depths of her she wanted to repent. She wanted to make him play his heavenly role and bestow forgiveness upon her. In the women's meeting she heard the voice of the young woman. It resembled her own voice when she was the same age, except that then she did not conceal her mouth with her hand like she was doing. She opened her lips wide and swallowed the black particles as if they were nothing.

'In the absence of pregnancy, the woman plays the role of mother, makes the man a child and bestows on him a role to play.'

She did not know why her stomach was not getting larger. His four women had also reached their menopause. They raised their hands to heaven pleading to become pregnant. They called on all the prophets and saints by name. None of them responded to them. They called on the Lady of Purity and other female saints, all to no avail.

'Is the man the cause?'

'Impossible. What have men got to do with women becoming pregnant?'

Under her ribs she felt the muscle trembling. In her head another muscle excreted thoughts. This black foam on her face was perhaps the surfeit of motherly tenderness, or perhaps it was a yearning for her mother's womb.

'Had her mother been buried alive in the bowels of the earth? Was this what pushed her to dig with her chisel, even though it's impossible?'

It was possible for her to orbit around the earth while she was lying down, and then return to the same spot where she had been. The man was there as well. He had just returned from work. His face was pale, and the black spots on his face had become blacker.

'Have you denounced me?'

'What do you mean?'

'I know that you are burning with desire to take revenge on me, but I warn you that we are partners in all things. In fact, it was you who always used to incite me against His Majesty. I was resisting your efforts to entice me with all my strength. If I gave in to you one day, that was only because I had despaired of reforming you. Yes indeed, you are a twisted rib that can only be repaired by breaking it.'

Her breast ceased to move and she began to choke. He was a man without pride. In her old life, he had more manhood. She wanted to cry out words, which were imprisoned but which she longed to be rid of. Words that she had to pronounce before the end of the world. Distasteful words, whose flavour made her sick, which women mumbled in bed with a man, when the heat was intense enough to melt shame, and vice was turned into virtue with a movement of a man's lips.

'I don't want anybody to know what happened. One day we shall be able to forget everything and celebrate His Majesty's birthday together. Put your hand in mine.'

His arm was stretched out towards her like a long stick. Before she stretched out her hand, he had grabbed it with his fingers. Big fingers covered in stains and calluses on skin the colour of oil.

In the night she tried to free her hand from his, but in vain. She turned over on her other side so that she was facing the wall. 'OK then, I'll run away tomorrow when he goes out to work.'

She fell asleep gazing at the wall. She saw herself sitting on the bridge waiting for the lights to appear. Silence fell as it became completely dark, then points of light began to appear from afar, multiplying as if they were reproducing by the thousands and millions. As numberless as the stars, gathering in a white beam, which hovered on the horizon and came to land on the roof. The Lady of Purity whispered in her ears, 'Hello there! What have you done up to now? Are you going to go on lying there like a sick cow?'

She pulled herself out from under the cover. The storm was throwing up black dust. A torrent pouring from heaven and from the bowels of the earth. The men were filling the jars. She could see them from afar on the skyline like little black shadows the size of children. They were moving their arms in the air as if they were playing, trying to empty the waters of the sea into little buckets, or to empty the air of heaven into a tin carafe.

She twisted her neck in an effort to see the women. The jar remained firmly on her head. No drops fell from it any more, even when she moved her head. To reach the women she had to slip down the slope covered with the muddy oil. She stopped halfway. She looked towards the horizon to the black dunes and to the blacker patches of the houses at the base of the dunes, and the roofs drowning in darkness, covered with overturned jars and dovecotes of black-feathered pigeons resembling bats, and the tips of minarets and the headstones of graves like raised crosses. She did not know the name of this village that she happened to find herself in. They called it Alma Mater. OK. What Alma Mater could this be, in which she was burying her head?

The women raised their arms. They despatched the jars with a strong movement of their necks and a bend of the upper part of their bodies. They sat on the edge of a rock covered with black moss. The earth was moist. The silence was as noisy as a wind whistling. Under the faint light the surface of the lake was covered with waves, waves that followed one another and piled up in crannies with the mosses. The dunes surrounded the place like walls blocking out the whole world that lay beyond them.

She was sitting in the middle, as her aunt used to sit in the middle of the women. One of them took a folded paper out of the pocket of her *jallaba*. The letters were in black ink in the handwriting of her husband or her boss at work, and of course it bore the seal of His Majesty.

The women craned their necks to read it. The letters were strange like the feet of the cockroaches of the black night.

'This is terrible.'

'Is there any way to rescue her?'

'To help her to run away?'

'Ah but. . .'

At this word the ladies shut their mouths in silence. A sound was heard like suppressed breathing, a feverish wind emerging from the breast, or perhaps the sound of the withdrawal of breath from the body. Her lips let out something like a cry. Of course, all of us need to run away, but where, when the world is empty? Before, yes, before, I used frequently to use this word' solidarity'. But it is forbidden to utter this word, as if it is Satan or the goddess of death Sekhmet.

'Sakhmutt?'

'We must correct people's pronunciation. We can do this because it is our tongues that utter words.'

'We shall not be worthy of a right that we take from hands other than our own.'

'Thus we allow ourselves to be put in situations that an animal would not accept.'

'There are only a limited number of things that we can do with our own hands.'

'Running away for instance?'

'We shall run away on our own feet, and not on anybody else's feet. That is clear.'

'And the travel ticket.'

'Ah yes, the ticket!'

'We must demand our wages.'

They all shouted with one voice. The word became like a ball of light that jumped from mouth to mouth, banging against the wall of darkness and returning in retreat carried by the wind to mouths that were still open, returning to where it was before it had been uttered. Silence fell.

'Haven't we demanded our wages before?'

'Yes, we have.'

'Then we must stop demanding them and take them with our own hands.'

The women exchanged glances behind the black cover. They scratched their heads where the skin had swollen under the base of the jars. Not one muscle of their faces moved. Their lips let out no sound. Their eyes darted backwards and forwards without seeing anything. She looked at the lake covered in dust. The moss in the crannies was being swept away by the current. The lake seemed to be as deep as the sea or the ocean, with dead bodies lying on the bottom.

'Is there someone watching us?'

The eye was looking out through the keyhole. She knew him immediately from his back view. The hump stood out under the faint light. The women raised their arms with one powerful movement. The jars returned to their places and settled in the holes on their heads. She could no longer see anything apart from their bowed backs. Their bodies were as small as children's, and their size decreased as they got further away, and there was no noise apart from the whispering of the *jallabas* in the distance like the rustling of the wind.

She was sitting by herself. The darkness of the night was growing less. The darkness had been veiling her like a curtain, and now the light was uncovering her. She saw the man standing there. She realised that he had seen her, as she had previously seen him. They were standing there, equal in their vision and height. This upright situation should not happen in a world that was not upright.

'You no longer have an opportunity.'

He said it angrily. By anger he was trying to conceal his lack of uprightness. It was her last opportunity, and if it were lost, there would not be another. She raised her arm to protect her face from the slap. If she did not raise it now, she would not raise it later. If she lived, she would live with her head held high. If she died, she would die kicking. She would not stop kicking until her last breath.

'This woman is losing blood.'

Indeed, the women needed to lose blood. If not, the world would remain as it was, and everything would end in nothing. We must take the fresh blood of this woman and transfuse it into the world that is on the point of death.

'She has finally closed her eyes and died, standing there like a tree.'

She remained standing in her place, incapable of movement. Her roots were in the bowels of the earth, her head was held high, tossed about by the wind. Her leaves trembled and her arms bent and twisted like twigs. She tried to no avail to rid herself of her branches. The wind rubbed against her audibly and with a regular rhythm like the breathing of someone sleeping.

'Will you go back to sleep in this heat?' he asked her in a voice full of jealousy. As if he was jealous of her ability to sleep. The gushing of the oil was eating away at the wall, and jealousy was eating away a bit of his flesh under the twisted rib. He jumped up, taking off his clothes as if he was stripping off his skin.

'I can stand it no longer. I have a desire.'

'To write?'

'Yes.'

'You have this new machine now, and you no longer need to know how to read or write.'

'Yes, but His Majesty wants a speech for his birthday tomorrow.'

'OK. The new machine can make a copy of last year's speech in a few minutes, can't it?'

'Yes, I know that.'

'What's new then?'

She grasped everything instinctively. Emptiness was spreading in the depths of her. What was the point of pretending then? There was no need to hide. Perhaps there was still some passion between them, the remains of a love from her old life. But there was a gust of wind and the current of oil swept everything away.

She heard the sound of the policeman typing and spinning in his swivel-chair.

'As you see, the woman went on leave.'

'Yes. These cases have become totally commonplace. One in three women goes on leave like this.'

'Is it a new illness?'

'Yes. In psychiatry, we call it schizophrenia.' As he said 'in psychiatry', he twisted his neck towards heaven at a sharp angle, and the pipe, which was fixed in the corner of his mouth, shook.

'Do you mean a dual personality?'

'No. With a dual personality, the woman and the other person are two who are forced to accompany one another. With schizophrenia, the woman herself and that other man become one person. Understood?'

'Yes. I know that. But the result is the same in any case.'

'Of course, but dual personality is a totally natural case, and all women can be put in this category.'

'Of course. I know that. Apart from our wives, of course.'

'Of course. Because we men are different from all other men. We are descended from a distinct lineage that stretches back to the prophets. Didn't you hear the speech of His Majesty on the occasion of his birthday?'

'Yes, I heard it. It was a historic speech, and I wrote that in my article in the newspaper. His Majesty must have seen it.'

'He must have seen the photographs at least. For as you know, His Majesty does not know how to read.'

'Yes, I know, and there is no shame in that. None of the prophets knew how to read, but in spite of that they led the world into a new era.'

'Yes, I know that, but His Majesty loves colour pictures, especially pictures of himself. He never gets bored of looking at pictures of himself published in the newspapers or broadcast on the screen, does he?'

'Of course he doesn't. That's natural for a great person like him who is leading us to the new oil era.'

'Of course, but what is the problem with oil?'

'Nothing except ...'

'Except what?'

'Nothing.'

'I feel that you want to say something. Come on, speak, don't be afraid.'

'Not at all. It was only a trivial thing. When I returned from work today I found a small paper.'

'A small paper?'

'Yes, a small paper on the chair near the bed.'

'That's right, on the chair near the bed. I know that.'

'How do you know?'

A deathly silence fell. All that could be heard was the hum of the fan, and the heavy breathing of the pair of them. Then the voice of one of them came faintly from afar as if from the bowels of the earth.

'What did she write to you on the paper?'

'Nothing important. Just that she had gone on holiday. That's all there is to it.'

'Is it really?'

'Yes, that's all there is to it.'

'I also found a paper.'

A deathly silence fell once again. The air stopped moving. The fan also stopped humming. Even their breathing seemed to stop.

She moved her head from on the pillow. The man was lying down with his eyes open. Suddenly laughter rang out in the darkness of the night. He was definitely the man who was laughing, definitely. Perhaps by his laughter he was concealing something else. He was facing the wall, and she did not know what he was thinking. But when she heard him laughing, she laughed as well, and life seemed to be better than it had been previously.

As long as he has the ability to laugh, there is no call to run away, at least not tonight. She can go on sleeping and tomorrow she will try again.

Also Available by NAWAL EL SAADAWI

Memoirs of a Woman Doctor

Distinguished literary critic Bodour is trapped in a loveless marriage and carries with her a dark secret. She fell in love in her youth and gave birth to an illegitimate daughter, Zeina, whom she abandoned on the streets of Cairo.

Bodour doesn't know that Zeina has blossomed into one of Egypt's most beloved entertainers. Pining for her estranged daughter, she writes a fictional account of her life in an attempt to find solace. But as the revolution in Cairo begins to gain fire, the novel goes missing and Bodour must find who has stolen it. Will her hunt for the thief bring mother and daughter together? Or is Bodour destined to lose her daughter to Cairo forever?

'El Saadawi is a superb stylist. This short book, one of her finest achievements, is nakedly inspirational in the impact of its heroine's revolt' *Morning Star*

'A powerfully written but simple account of an independent woman's search for identity in a traditional society' *British Medical Journal*

978 0 86356 610 3   £8.99

Also Available by NAWAL EL SAADAWI

Zeina

Distinguished literary critic Bodour is trapped in a loveless marriage and carries with her a dark secret. She fell in love in her youth and gave birth to an illegitimate daughter, Zeina, whom she abandoned on the streets of Cairo.

Bodour doesn't know that Zeina has blossomed into one of Egypt's most beloved entertainers. Pining for her estranged daughter, she writes a fictional account of her life in an attempt to find solace. But as the revolution in Cairo begins to gain fire, the novel goes missing and Bodour must find who has stolen it. Will her hunt for the thief bring mother and daughter together? Or is Bodour destined to lose her daughter to Cairo forever?

'An uncompromising attack on patriarchy, power and hypocrisy in modern-day Egypt.' *The Times*

'Read this novel to grasp the bravery of El Saadawi's activism in Egypt and to learn more about her country' *The Guardian*

978 0 86356 355 3   £8.99

Also Available by NAWAL EL SAADAWI

Two Women in One

Bahiah Shaheen is an eighteen-year-old medical student and daughter of a prominent Egyptian public official. She finds the male students in her class rough, coarse and alien. Her father, too, seems to belong to a race apart, and the Bahia has long ceased to be surprised at not being her real self in his presence. But what, she wonders, is this real self?

At an exhibition of some of her paintings, a stranger engages Bahiah in conversation. This proves to be the beginning of Bahiah's road to self-discovery as she abandons the life constructed for her.

'These two women live, to some degree, in every thinking woman.' *New York Times Book Review*

'The story represents the lives of thousands of women but here it is also fiercely individual, thanks to Nawal El-Saada-wi's spikily stylised treatment ... bitingly to the point' *New Statesman*

978 0 86356 562 5   £7.99

Also Available by **NAWAL EL SAADAWI**

The Fall of the Imam

Bint Allah knows herself only as the Daughter of God. Born in a stifling male-dominated state ruled by the Imam and his coterie of ministers, she dreams of one day reaching the top of a distant hill visible through the bars of the orphanage window.

But nothing escapes the attention of the Imam who is never satisfied no matter what he consumes, and who never feels secure no matter how well he protects himself. When the Imam falsely accuses Bint Allah of adultery and sentences her to death by stoning, he is not prepared for the unexpected repercussions that follow.

This powerful, poetic novel reveals the underlying hypocrisy of male-dominated religious states, and the insufferable predicament of women in a society that must ultimately self-destruct.

'Haunting and mesmerising' *New Humanist*

'A feminist fantasy narrative' *The International Fiction Review*

978 1 84659 062 7 £7.99

SAQI BOOKSHE/F

Saqi has been publishing innovative writers from the Middle East and beyond since 1983. Our new Saqi Bookshelf series brings together a curated list of the most dazzling works from this kaleidoscopic region, from bold, original voices and contemporary bestsellers, to modern classics. Begin collecting your Saqi Bookshelf and discover the world around the corner.

For more reading recommendations, new books and discounts, join the conversation here: